MISSION RECOVERY
"SPECIAL OPERATIONS"

Director: Thomas Casey
Deputy Director: Lucas Camp

When all else fails,
a Specialist is called in to "recover" a situation.

This team of highly skilled men and women was created to serve the needs of all other U.S. government agencies whenever the usual channels failed. The elite force is trained in every area of antiterrorism and aggressive infiltration. All agents have extensive stealth and sniper training and are multilingual. They must meet the most stringent mental and physical requirements of any national or international security force. They are prepared to do *whatever* it takes to accomplish their mission....

Failure is *not* an option.

Dear Harlequin Intrigue Reader,

Yeah, it's cold outside, but we have just the remedy to heat you up—another fantastic lineup of breathtaking romantic suspense!

Getting things started with even more excitement than usual is Debra Webb with a super spin-off of her popular COLBY AGENCY series. THE SPECIALISTS is a trilogy of ultradaring operatives the likes of which are rarely—if ever—seen. And man, are they sexy! Look for *Undercover Wife* this month and two more thrillers to follow in February and March. Hang on to your seats.

A triple pack of TOP SECRET BABIES also kicks off the New Year. First out: *The Secret She Keeps* by Cassie Miles. Can you imagine how you'd feel if you learned the father of your child was back...as were all the old emotions? This one, by a veteran Harlequin Intrigue author, is surely a keeper. Promotional titles by Mallory Kane and Ann Voss Peterson respectively follow in the months to come.

And since Cupid is once again a blip on the radar screen, we thought we'd highlight some special Valentine picks for the holiday. Harper Allen singes the sheets so to speak with *McQueen's Heat* and Adrianne Lee is *Sentenced To Wed* this month. Next month, Amanda Stevens fans the flames with *Confessions of the Heart*. **WARNING:** You may need sunblock to read these scorchers.

Enjoy!

Sincerely,

Denise O'Sullivan
Associate Senior Editor
Harlequin Intrigue

UNDERCOVER WIFE

DEBRA WEBB

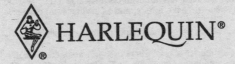

HARLEQUIN®

TORONTO • NEW YORK • LONDON
AMSTERDAM • PARIS • SYDNEY • HAMBURG
STOCKHOLM • ATHENS • TOKYO • MILAN • MADRID
PRAGUE • WARSAW • BUDAPEST • AUCKLAND

ISBN 0-373-22693-4

UNDERCOVER WIFE

This edition published by arrangement with Harlequin Books S.A.

® and TM are trademarks of the publisher. Trademarks indicated with
® are registered in the United States Patent and Trademark Office, the
Canadian Trade Marks Office and in other countries.

Visit us at www.eHarlequin.com

Printed in U.S.A.

ABOUT THE AUTHOR

Debra Webb was born in Scottsboro, Alabama, to parents who taught her that anything is possible if you want it badly enough. She began writing at age nine. Eventually she met and married the man of her dreams and tried some other occupations, including selling vacuum cleaners and working in a factory, a day-care center, a hospital and a department store. When her husband joined the military, they moved to Berlin, Germany, and Debra became a secretary in the commanding general's office. By 1985 they were back in the States, and finally moved to Tennessee, to a small town where everyone knows everyone else. With the support of her husband and two beautiful daughters, Debra took up writing again, looking to mystery and movies for inspiration. In 1998 her dream of writing for Harlequin came true. You can write to Debra with your comments at P.O. Box 64, Huntland, Tennessee 37345.

Books by Debra Webb

HARLEQUIN INTRIGUE

HARLEQUIN AMERICAN ROMANCE

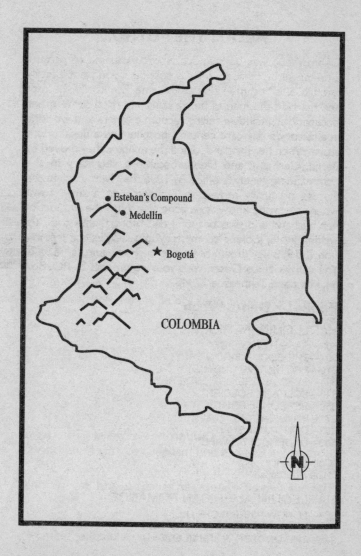

Esteban's Compound

Medellín

★ Bogotá

COLOMBIA

N

CAST OF CHARACTERS

Erin Bailey—Wrongly imprisoned for a crime she did not commit, Erin is desperate to regain her freedom and her life. But can she trust the handsome stranger who makes her an offer that sounds too good to be true?

John Logan—A specialist in a highly covert government organization, can he accomplish the mission no one else has been able to, and keep his "new" partner alive at the same time?

Thomas Casey—The enigmatic director of Mission Recovery.

Lucas Camp—Deputy director of Mission Recovery. He will do whatever is necessary to take care of his specialists. His people are his number one priority.

Pablo Esteban—A brutal and infamous drug smuggler and gunrunner. He hires only the best and only couples. *No one* disappoints Esteban.

Maria Esteban—Pablo's sister. He protects her to the extent that she is all but a prisoner in her own home.

Larry and Sheila Watters—A couple who want to remain number one in Esteban's eyes. They will stop at nothing to keep that position.

Hector and Carlos Caldarone—Brothers who have worked for Esteban and managed to stay alive longer than anyone else.

Vincent Ferrelli—Another specialist, and Logan's only backup in Colombia.

Ramon and Maverick—Two top members of Mission Recovery's Detail and Housekeeping Team.

This book is dedicated to all the American men and women who risk their lives every day to keep our country safe and free in too many capacities to name. God bless you all.

Chapter One

"What's so important that it couldn't wait until I reported in day after tomorrow?" John Logan dropped into one of the upholstered chairs flanking the director's desk. He and his partner hadn't taken any real time off in over eight months. They were due some serious R&R—past due. This little trip back to D.C. hadn't been on Logan's agenda for the day.

He forced himself to relax. The jet lag was definitcly catching up to him. Or, he thought wryly, maybe it was last night's margaritas. A smile hitched his lips when he considered the private party he'd had with that sweet little senorita. Too bad this morning's predawn wake-up call had dragged him from the rumpled bed before they'd had the opportunity to share an encore.

"We have a problem." Lucas Camp, Deputy Director of Mission Recovery's Special Operations, leaned against the edge of Director Casey's desk, his solemn gaze resting on Logan.

The undercurrent in Lucas's tone tugged Logan's wayward thoughts back to the here and now. Uneasiness tightened in his chest. He knew that tone, that look. Lucas was searching for the best way to say what needed to be said. Whatever it was, it wasn't good.

Logan straightened in his chair, instantly running down a list of possible scenarios. "What kind of problem?"

Director Thomas Casey stepped into the dim pool of light provided by the brass lamp on his desk. The man always lingered in the shadows. As new to the organization as he was, Casey had already garnered himself a reputation for the cloak-and-dagger routine.

Logan, his senses rushing toward full-scale alert, shifted his attention to Casey. Something big was about to go down.

"We may have to abort the South American mission." Casey's gaze pierced Logan's with the intensity of twin blue laser beams. "Taylor is dead."

Dead?

Logan was on his feet with no memory of how he'd gotten there. Jess Taylor was his partner. They had parted company just forty-eight hours ago to take some quick downtime before their mission began. How could she be dead? Logan shook his head in denial. There had to be a mistake.

"We just—she was..." Logan's voice faltered beneath the steady gazes fixed on him. There was no way either of these two men, his superiors, would lie to him. "How?" He barely recognized the harsh sound as his own voice.

"Sanchez hit her outside the airport in L.A.," Lucas said quietly. "We know it was him because there were three eyewitnesses. Based on the description, there's no question."

Fury roared inside Logan. Sanchez, the weasel son of a bitch. Logan should have killed him when he had the chance. But Sanchez had begged for mercy and sworn that he would spill his guts about the drug runners trafficking for the Mexican kingpin Mission Recovery had worked to bring down for nearly a year. Jess had fallen, hook, line and sinker, for Sanchez's act. Logan hadn't trusted him, but he had deferred to Jess's judgment. Now he was sorry. But not half as sorry as Sanchez would be.

"Where is he?"

Lucas raised an eyebrow at the savage sound of Logan's demand. "We're taking care of Sanchez."

"*I'll* take care of Sanchez," Logan countered. His muscles tightened with rage. He wanted to tear something apart. He wanted to watch Sanchez die slowly, very, very slowly.

"You already have your assignment," Casey pointed out in that calm, even manner of his that represented nothing more than another of his illusions.

Thomas Casey was one hundred percent lethal and completely heartless. The mission was always his top priority. That was the way of things in Mission Recovery, the most highly covert organization belonging to the United States government. Created to serve the needs of all other government agencies, CIA, FBI, ATF, DEA, whenever the usual channels failed, Mission Recovery was called in to "recover" the situation. The elite group of specialists were highly trained in all areas of anti-terrorism and aggressive infiltration. When all else failed, a specialist was sent in to salvage things. This was one of those times. But Jess's death had changed everything.

Logan aimed his fury in Casey's direction then. "Jess is dead. It's going to be pretty damned hard to complete that mission now. No partner, no pass into Esteban's tight little group. It was a package deal, remember? Couples only."

"We may have an alternative." Lucas opened the folder lying next to him on Casey's desk. "Erin Bailey." He tapped an eight-by-ten picture that made Logan do a double take.

The mane of thick hair was too long and blond instead of black, the lips a little fuller maybe, but otherwise the woman in the photograph could have been Jess in disguise.

"Who the hell is she?" Logan's focus never left the photograph. The curve of her cheek, the delicate line of her nose, and the extraordinary violet eyes were exactly the same. It was unnerving…eerie.

"It gets better," Lucas added knowingly, anticipation lifting his tone. "She's a hacker, U.S. Grade A. Not in the usual sense, however, she specializes in computer security. Learned her hacking skills to better serve her needs as a security analyst."

Computers? That had been Jess's specialty. That particular skill was necessary to the success of the South American mission. "How'd you find her?"

"Completely by accident," Lucas explained. "Forward Research found her."

Logan knew all about Forward Research. The group was composed of a dozen men and women who did nothing but recon for people who showed unparalleled skill in a given field. It was Forward Research who had discovered Logan three years ago. Now he was a specialist who met the most stringent mental and physical requirements of any national or international security force.

Putting his fury on hold momentarily to assuage his morbid curiosity, he asked, "Have you recruited her?"

"No." Casey answered the question. "First, we wanted to see if you would have a problem with this approach."

Yeah, right. Casey didn't give one damn if Logan had a problem with it or not. If the woman could be gotten, the mission would go on.

"We know you don't want to let all the months of hard work you and Jess put into this mission go down the proverbial drain," Lucas said, placating him. "Erin Bailey is our only hope for salvaging this mission."

Logan wanted to say to hell with the mission, Jess was dead. But an instinct too strongly entrenched wouldn't allow him to do that. This mission *was* top priority. If their circumstances were reversed, Jess would feel the same.

"Where is she?" Logan asked roughly.

"In an Atlanta federal penitentiary."

Logan looked from Lucas to the haunting photograph and back. "What'd she do?" The innocent-looking woman in the picture hardly looked capable of criminal activity. Another strike against her, Logan mused. How in the hell would she ever survive in Esteban's world?

"Nothing, she says." Amusement twinkled in Lucas's eyes. "But then, all prisoners say that."

"She tampered with the security systems of several large southeast corporations in order to drum up business for the small but rising cyber security company where she worked," Casey explained. "She was sentenced to five years. She's only served four months of her term and, from recent accounts, isn't faring so well with prison life."

A look passed between Lucas and Casey. Logan would just bet that the Bailey woman's run of bad luck in her new prison life had more to do with Mission Recovery than fate. Mission Recovery liked to stack their deck.

Whatever the case, Logan picked up the folder and stared more closely at Erin Bailey. According to the accompanying physical description, she was approximately the same height and weight as Jess. Five-two, one hundred five pounds. He frowned. "Does she have any family? A boyfriend, maybe, who might create a problem?"

Lucas shook his head. "Not a soul. She was apparently engaged to her boss when she got busted. He swore under oath that he knew nothing of her criminal activities. I don't think he misses her, considering the brunette hanging on his arm these days."

Something about that little story didn't sit right with Logan, but the woman's personal problems weren't his concern. "What makes you think she'll go for it?" He leveled his gaze on Casey's. "We all know just how much risk is involved."

"Erin Bailey wants her life back." Casey reached across his desk and took the folder from Logan. He fanned through the pages until he found the one he wanted. He glanced over it, then closed the folder and dropped it back onto the polished surface of his mahogany desk. "And I'd be willing to wager she wouldn't turn down the opportunity for a little revenge. We already know that her boyfriend set her up. But, just in case she's not interested, we've set a little incentive in motion. It's all in the file." Casey smiled, a gesture that made him seem almost human. "I've made arrangements for you to offer her a deal."

Logan tensed inwardly. He wondered if the Bailey woman would be foolish enough to make a deal with the devil himself. But Logan wasn't going to waste any time or energy trying to figure out who represented the biggest threat to Erin Bailey, Esteban or Mission Recovery.

"And if she accepts our offer?" Logan suggested.

The smile dissolved into the usual grim line that Logan associated with the unit's new director. "Then you have one week to turn Erin Bailey into Jessica Taylor."

ERIN WAS DREAMING. She was standing in the middle of a beautiful green meadow. Bluebonnets and daisies were sprinkled amid the sea of lush green. A wide-open blue sky spilled from the heavens as far as the eye could see, with only a puff of white here and there to disrupt the absolute infinity of pure blue color.

In the dream, Erin closed her eyes and spun around slowly. The tall grass tickled her ankles. It felt soft beneath her bare feet. The sweet smell was all around her. The scent of wildflowers...of rich, green grass... the smell of freedom—

"On your feet."

Erin jolted awake, squinted through the darkness and tried to make out the silhouette hovering over her cot. Fear surged through her when a strong hand closed over her shoulder and shook her. Oh, God, what if Guard Roland had decided to make good on his threat? Or was it that inmate who seemed to have it in for her? Panic tightened around Erin's chest. She wanted to scream, but the sound simply knotted in her throat.

"What—what're you doing?" she managed to mumble around the lump of fear. It was well past midnight. The cellblock was deathly quiet.

"I said, *on your feet,*" the gruff voice repeated in a harsh whisper.

The voice was different. This wasn't the guard who had threatened her. Relief washed over Erin as she scrambled from beneath the threadbare covers. Feeling her way, she pushed her feet into her shoes, stood and quickly righted her rumpled clothes.

The guard tugged first one hand then the other in front of her and handcuffed her wrists together. "Keep your mouth shut. I don't want you waking up the whole damned block."

He shined his flashlight in her face. Erin squeezed her eyes shut against the blinding light and nodded her understanding. The light vanished with a definite *click*. Where was he taking her at this time of night? What did he want? She frowned. Why had he handcuffed her? Before she could consider the questions further, the guard pushed her through the door, then closed and locked it behind him.

The rasp of leather soles on the concrete was the only sound as they passed cell after cell. The occasional cough or snore from a sleeping inmate splintered the dark silence from time to time, but no one roused enough to wonder or witness what was happening to Inmate 541-22.

Erin wanted desperately to ask where they were going, but fear kept her silent. Too many times she had seen inmates pay the price for disobedience. The guard had told her to keep her mouth shut, and she would. But, God help her, fear thudded in her heart, leaped in her pulse. How could she trust anyone in this place? The near darkness of the long corridor only served to sharpen her awareness of being locked up. How would she ever survive another four years and eight months here? Even the confined, sweaty odor of the place made her sick to her stomach.

At the final checkpoint, another guard opened the door leading from the cellblock. A dim circle of light from the desk lamp lit the female guard's unsmiling features. The door slammed shut behind Erin and ''her escort,'' leaving her both relieved and anxious. Inside that cell she felt relatively safe from the evil that existed all around her, but at the same time she felt this pathetic world closing in on her in that six-by-nine cinder-block room.

Before they reached the main visitors area, the guard hesitated in front of one of the doors leading to an interview room. The same room where Erin had met with her lawyer on the two occasions he'd seen fit to show interest in her case.

"I'll be waiting right here to take you back to your cell." His words more warning than statement of fact, he opened the door and waited for her to enter the room.

"I don't understand." Erin felt the sudden, unbidden urge to run. "Why am I here?"

"Go on." The guard gestured to the door. "You have a visitor." This time his tone was clearly impatient, annoyed.

A visitor? For her? Had Jeff, the bastard, come to apologize? To tell her that this whole thing had been a huge misunderstanding? That she was free to go now? Erin almost laughed at that. He had used her. She gritted her teeth at the pain still simmering beneath the barely controlled surface she maintained. He had ruined her life, her career. Everything. She would never work in a position that required a security clearance again. And he had come out of the whole mess smelling like a rose. She had taken the fall for him. All his promises had been nothing more than lies.

Now she was paying the price for her naïveté.

Erin squared her shoulders and took a deep breath. Whoever was here to see her in the middle of the night, it wouldn't be Jeff. It wouldn't be her lawyer either. He had told her she was doomed from the beginning. Of course, Jeff had been the one who hired him. She had been such a fool.

The door closed with a loud *clang* behind her. Erin jerked at the sound of it locking. God, how she hated being locked up. As if on cue, the walls began to close in on her. How would she ever endure the remainder of her sentence? Her breath came in quick, shallow puffs. Fate and Jeff had left her without any choice. She was a prisoner and no one was going to rescue her as she'd foolishly prayed during her first month in this horrible place.

Calm down, she ordered herself. Focus on anything else. This room. She'd been here before. But this time it was only dimly lit. Since it was the middle of the night, no light shone in through the window on the far wall. A singular bulb spilled its sparse light over the empty table in the center of the room. The two mismatched chairs were vacant.

"Have a seat."

Startled, Erin turned toward the sound of the voice. She didn't recognize the tall, dark-haired man who stepped into the pool of light near the table. He'd been waiting there and she hadn't even noticed. And she would definitely have remembered meeting a man as handsome as this one. Five o'clock shadow darkened his chin and chiseled jaw. The white cotton shirt he wore was a bit wrinkled. His jeans were slightly faded, worn enough to be comfortable. He looked rumpled, as if he had traveled a very long way or had just awakened and pulled on the same clothes he'd worn the day before.

Since he made no effort to introduce himself Erin didn't ask. She crossed the room and settled into the chair on her side of the table that stood between them. She was a prisoner, without any rights to speak of. When she was told to jump, she did so. Erin had no intention of doing anything that might keep her in this place one minute longer than necessary.

The man sat down and began flipping through the file on the table before him. "My name is John Logan, Ms. Bailey, I've come here to offer you a proposition." His gaze settled on hers then, watching, analyzing.

His eyes were disturbing, too seeing, and so brown they were almost black. Erin tamped down the anticipation that welled inside her. She would not get her hopes up that this man could somehow rescue her from the living hell her bad choices had plunged her into.

"It's the middle of the night," she countered. "Isn't this an awfully odd hour to discuss business, Mr. Logan?"

Erin had learned the hard way that business conducted after hours was usually a little shady. Besides, she didn't know this man. What kind of proposition could he possibly want to offer her? Could he be from the district attorney's office? Maybe they had decided that pursuing Jeff was worthwhile after all. But her visitor's manner of dress and the fact that it was definitely past business hours seemed to negate that possibility.

He closed the file and leaned back in his chair to assess her. Erin held his gaze. She would not give him the satisfaction of looking away. She was in prison, for God's sake, what else could he do to her? Then she remembered the threats lurking within these very walls and she shuddered. There were too many despicable and degrading possibilities to consider.

"You've only completed four months of your sentence." He scrubbed a hand over his jaw as if he were tired, and had no patience for any of this. "Five years is a very long time, Ms. Bailey."

Erin twisted her right wrist inside the confining handcuffs. She still couldn't understand why the guard handcuffed her for this meeting. She wasn't a violent inmate. And she could definitely count. "I'm very much aware of the time I'm facing, Mr. Logan."

He leaned forward, pressing her with that unsettling gaze. "Then I wouldn't be complaining about what time of day or night my one hope for freedom came."

Freedom? Who was this man? What was he talking about? "Who sent you here?" she demanded, afraid to believe his words and equally scared not to. The false hope his insinuations engendered in her was too cruel for words.

"I can't tell you that." He folded his arms on the table, covering the file that likely contained information about her. "And even if I told you, you wouldn't know any more than you do now."

"I don't understand." For the first time since stepping into the room, fear for her safety rocketed through Erin. Was the guard still outside as he had said he would be? "I think I should go back to my cell now."

She started to stand, but his next words stopped her.

"I can make all this go away."

That was impossible. "How can you do that?" she demanded, knowing full well it couldn't be true. She lifted her chin and glared at him, daring him to prove his statement.

"The people I work for are very powerful. If you cooperate with us, they *will* clear your record. You'll be free to resume your life in any way you see fit."

That sounded too good to be true. There had to be a catch. "And what do I have to do in exchange?" She surveyed the angular features of his handsome face, lines and angles, shadow and light. His expression gave nothing away, nor did those dark, dark eyes. How could she trust him? No matter how good-looking he was, or how important he appeared to be. She didn't know him. He was a stranger. A stranger with enough power to waltz into a federal prison in the middle of the night and have the guards at his beck and call. That realization sent a chill straight to her bones.

He studied her for a while before he responded to her question. "We need you for a mission that involves national security. You will assume someone else's identity, and you'll be working very closely with me. Without you, the mission will have to be aborted."

National security? Someone else's identity? "Whose identity?" She had to be dreaming. This couldn't be real. Stuff like this only happened in the movies.

"You'll be briefed on everything you need to know before the mission begins." He lifted a briefcase from the floor and placed it on the table. Once he'd opened it, he placed the file inside, then closed the case and stood. He leveled his gaze back on hers. "Any questions?"

"Wait." She resisted the urge to reach out to him, touch him…just to see if he was real. This was all far too unbelievable. Surely he couldn't expect her to make a decision based on so little information. She had to know more. "I can't make a decision without more details than what you've given me. And I'll need time to think it over."

Impatience pounded in the muscle jerking in his tightly clenched jaw. "We don't have *time*. If you choose to cooperate, you will do exactly what I tell you, when I tell you. There will be no discussion." He lifted the briefcase from the table. "Now, are you in or out?"

Erin shook her head. This was crazy. "What kind of mission? Where?"

"I can't answer either of those questions. You will be given that information on a need to know basis, and right now you know all you need to. What's your decision?"

A mixture of irritation and fear fueled Erin. "You can't expect me to just say yes. There are things I have to know and consider."

"Like what?" He cocked his handsome head and

glared at her. "Like whether or not you'll survive if Inmate Evans decides she wants to do to you what she did to that judge in Savannah?" He lifted a speculative eyebrow. "Or maybe you want to contemplate Guard Roland's next move as the months and years of your sentence crawl by."

How could he know those things? No one knew. She hadn't told anyone. "Who are you?"

"I'm your fairy godfather, Erin Bailey. I can make your greatest wish come true. I can clear your name, and I can make your old friend Jeff pay for his evil deeds." Logan stared directly into her eyes for two beats before he turned and strode away. He didn't stop until he reached the door. He glanced back at her, his expression challenging, openly condescending. "Are you in or out?"

Erin swallowed the fear climbing into her throat. What if he was right? What if this was her one chance for freedom? *I can make all this go away.* The mere thought of Jeff getting his due made her giddy.

"There's one thing I have to know," she insisted, delaying her answer though anticipation bubbled inside her at that last thought.

Irritation rolled off the handsome stranger in waves, but he waited for her question just the same.

"This mission you want me to help with, is it dangerous?"

Something changed in his eyes. All signs of cockiness and condescension drained from his expression. Erin's heart hammered violently in the silent seconds that elapsed before he answered.

"Very."

The solitary word echoed around her, filling her with renewed desperation. His gaze never leaving hers, he pounded once on the door. It opened instantly. He walked out, leaving the door wide open. Allowing her to make her own decision.

In or out.

Chapter Two

Two little words. *I'm in.*

Logan had stared at her for what felt like an eternity, something vaguely like regret in those dark eyes, before he turned to the guard and informed him that he'd be taking Erin with him. The guard had immediately removed her handcuffs as if the warden himself had given the order. Heart still pounding, palms still sweating, and a full twenty minutes later she settled into the back seat of a large black SUV parked outside the main prison entrance. Every second of those twenty minutes had ticked by one by one in Erin's frantic mind. It didn't seem possible that it was really happening, but it was. She was free to go with this stranger who'd shown up in the middle of the night.

Logan closed her door then slid into the passenger seat next to the SUV's waiting driver.

"Airport?" the guy behind the wheel asked.

"Yeah."

The driver glanced at her in the rearview mirror, his gaze brief yet assessing. She shivered beneath that swift scrutiny, but quickly forced the uneasiness away.

She had to be strong. This was too important to allow fear to get in her way. She was out! Giddiness made her tremble. A few more feet and she would be clear of the last remaining barriers of incarceration.

The vehicle eased into forward motion, gaining speed as it rolled down the long drive. Erin held her breath as the massive prison gates opened and they passed through unimpeded. Relief so profound surged through her that she felt light-headed with the drugging effect of it.

Ten or so seconds later reality broadsided her. What had she agreed to do? Fear slithered up her spine, freezing the sweet sense of relief in her veins, as she considered that she was being driven into the darkness, toward the unknown, by two complete strangers. Twisting around in her seat, she stared at the gray prison walls and the security fence as they left both behind. A tiny seed of hope sprouted deep inside her at the realization that she was really leaving that awful place. This was not a dream, waking or sleeping. Whatever she'd signed on to do, it had started. She was out!

When the bright security lights were a dim glow in the distance she turned back to face front again. To face the consequences of the decision she'd made.

Gone was the prison garb she'd despised so. In its place she wore the jeans, T-shirt and sneakers she'd arrived in four months ago. The rest of her personal effects, ID, jewelry, pictures, etcetera, remained in a large padded envelope now in Logan's possession. He'd told her she wouldn't need them right now. A new thought occurred to her then. She chewed her lower lip as her anxiety spiked again. Had she traded one kind of prison for another? Where were they going? What would happen after they arrived?

"Why are we going to the airport?" Her voice sounded small in the oppressive silence. Surely they didn't expect to keep the intended destination a secret from her at this point.

"We have a plane to catch," Logan said without looking back at her. "That's all you need to know right now."

She opened her mouth to argue, but snapped it shut again. There was no point demanding answers when she knew he wouldn't give them. The last thing she wanted to do was antagonize the man since her fate lay squarely in his hands. The prison had signed over responsibility of her to him. She was in his charge, at his mercy.

Just like with Jeff.

She shuddered inwardly at the flash of memories that accompanied that last thought. No. That wasn't completely true. This man was nothing like her former fiancé. The information Logan had given her so far— paltry as it was—did appear to be the truth. He worked for the government, she was as certain as she could be of that. She'd seen his credentials and the jurisdiction paperwork when he'd signed for her release. No one at the prison—not even her, not really—had questioned anything. The idea of gaining her freedom once more had been far too tempting for her to think rationally.

But now those more rational thoughts wouldn't abate. He'd said he needed her for a mission that involved national security. She would assume someone else's identity. The mission was very dangerous. But what kind of expertise or experience could she offer this man or her country?

A new kind of stress churned inside her, turning her insides to ice, threatening to shatter her. She fought it. Hugged her arms around her middle and forced herself to remain calm, at least on the surface. She would have the answers she needed when the right time came. He'd assured her of that. There was no need for her to come unglued just yet.

She squared her shoulders and lifted her chin. Whatever it took to get her life back she would do it. She wasn't the trusting little naïve fool she'd been two years ago. She'd learned the hard way not to trust anyone, most especially a man who put his work before all else. Her gaze went automatically to the back of John Logan's dark head. A man like him, she knew instinctively. Well, she didn't have to trust him in that way. And she definitely had no plans to get to know him intimately. This was a business deal. All she had to do was follow his instructions and she'd have her life back. She wanted that more than she wanted to take her next breath.

Whatever happened tomorrow, one thing was irrefutable—right now, this minute, she was free again.

That would have to be enough.

She'd gotten through the last four months one day at a time, she'd get through this the same way.

To her surprise, they didn't go to Hartfield, Atlanta's International Airport, as Erin had assumed they would. Instead the driver parked near a hangar at Atlanta's favored alternate, PDK Airport. The plane, small jet actually, the kind corporate executives used, gleamed in the runway lights. She followed Logan and the driver in that direction. As far as she could see only one man waited nearby.

"We're fueled and ready for flight," the new man said to Logan. Almost as tall as Logan, he was older, but looked every bit as physically fit.

The pilot, Erin decided. Despite his rugged profile, he looked friendly enough. In her opinion, none of these guys really looked like secret agents. Well, except for Logan. He did have that aura of danger...a kind of sexy mystique. Then again, all she had to go by was what she'd seen in the movies. Probably not good examples, she decided.

Exhaustion and anxiety clawing at her frazzled nerves, she exhaled a loud, heavy breath. She hadn't meant to, it just came out, igniting instead of releasing a tide of new anxiety. Logan and the driver from the SUV turned simultaneously and stared at her. Erin swallowed, trying her level best not to let those piercing stares undo her already flimsy bravado.

After a moment that lasted far too long, Logan turned his attention back to the pilot. "We'll be ready in five."

The man, pilot, whatever, nodded and headed toward the plane. The SUV driver, who was slighter and somewhat shorter in build than the other two, followed. She decided that he was of Latin descent, though his English was perfect and was spoken with no accent at all.

Erin felt Logan's intense gaze on her long before she worked up the nerve to make eye contact. Unable to pretend not to notice any longer, she stiffened her spine and met that assessing gaze head-on. Whatever he expected of her she could do it, she told herself again. She *had* to do it.

"Last chance, Bailey. What's it going to be? You still in?"

How could he think she'd back out now? She'd come this far. She sure as heck wasn't returning to that prison. "Of course I'm still in," she said sharply, though her voice sounded a little shaky and a lot hollow to her own ears.

That dark, dark gaze bored deeply into hers. For just a second Erin was sure she saw concern, or something on that order, then he banished it.

"All right. But don't say I didn't offer you an out."

Before Erin could string together an appropriate retort, he turned and strode to the waiting jet. She blinked, suddenly uncertain of herself all over again. He'd given her one last chance to change her mind. She hadn't taken it. Was that a mistake? If she boarded that plane would she ever see Atlanta again? Was her passion for freedom going to be a death wish in the end?

There was no one she could turn to. No one who even cared, or who would miss her when she was gone. Her parents had died years ago. She had no siblings. And Jeff, well, he'd been a total jerk. He sure wouldn't miss her. The fact that she didn't have any friends to call upon was no one's fault but her own. She'd always been too busy with work. Work, work, work. That's all she'd done since graduating college three years ago. Now look at her. Following a complete stranger to God knows where to do only the Devil knew what.

Erin Bailey, this is your life.

And it sucked.

Logan paused a few feet away from the open boarding door. "It's the point of no return, Bailey. If you're still a go, don't look back because nothing about your life will ever be the same again."

She couldn't have replied even if she'd thought of something exceedingly witty to say. Her throat had closed with fear and a few other emotions she'd just as soon not analyze at the moment. In spite of it all, or maybe because of it, her feet moved her forward, toward the unknown. Toward this man who offered her everything and yet nothing at all.

He didn't have to worry, she wouldn't look back.

LESS THAN thirty minutes after liftoff from Atlanta's PDK Airport, Erin Bailey was sleeping like a baby. That shouldn't bother Logan, but it did. He'd seen the fear in her eyes the moment he offered her the *deal.* She'd hesitated, but the desire to have her freedom back was too great. She'd caved as readily as a sandcastle in the evening tide. Even the fact that he refused to answer her most elementary questions hadn't dissuaded her for more than a fleeting moment.

He'd given her one last chance to change her mind before they boarded the aircraft and she'd refused. What happened from this point forward was no longer his responsibility.

Yeah, right.

Like he could change how he felt about the players or this mission. It was dangerous, even for a seasoned undercover field operative. For Erin Bailey it was a suicide mission. On some level she recognized that cold hard fact. He'd seen the truth in her eyes back there on that landing strip. But she'd reined in her fear and climbed aboard anyway.

She was made out of stronger stuff than he'd first given her credit. He'd ordered her to get some sleep as soon as they hit cruising altitude. She'd obeyed, probably more from exhaustion than motivation to please him.

The next six days would provide the rest of the story. There wasn't time to teach her everything she needed to know. All Logan could hope for was to prevent a catastrophe by pushing her beyond all limits to see if she'd break. If she couldn't tolerate the pressure, she would get them both killed and blow any future prospects of getting close to Esteban. Testing her mental and physical strength was Logan's primary objective. He had to know just how much she could handle. Once she'd proven her ability to keep it together then he would give her an abbreviated course in illegal drugs and military weapons. It wasn't necessary that she know as much as Jess had, but it was crucial that she appear knowledgeable.

One wrong word, one wrong move in Esteban's or any of his people's presence and she was dead.

Logan closed his eyes and leaned back in his seat. God, he didn't want to do this, but there was simply no other way. Jess would do the same if she were still alive. It didn't seem right that she was gone. They'd worked together for three years. She was the best partner he'd ever had. He opened his eyes and turned his head toward his new, *temporary* partner whose looks and advanced computer skills had gotten her into this predicament.

Erin Bailey was pretty and soft in a more feminine way than Jess had been. But Bailey would never be able to match Jess's extraordinary skill as an operative—not in a week, not in three years, nor in a thousand. Bailey knew nothing of this life except the nonsense she'd likely seen in movies or read about in books. The life of an international spy was not nearly so glamorous and was far more dangerous than the entertainment industry portrayed it. If Bailey thought she was merely going to play a role in the latest James Bond film, she had a rude awakening coming.

She had no idea just how much danger she was in already and the mission hadn't even begun.

DAWN WAS STREAKING its way across the horizon as Erin half stumbled off the plane. Her legs felt weak and rubbery. It was hard to believe she'd slept the entire flight. She scrubbed the last vestiges of sleep from her eyes and tried to focus on her new, unfamiliar surroundings. Distant mountains were surrounded by desertlike terrain that sprawled for as far as the eye could see in the purple hues of dawn. The air smelled different. Fresher, yet thinner somehow.

"Where…" she cleared her throat "…where are we?"

Logan, sans briefcase, slowed his pace only long enough to toss a glance over his shoulder. "Mexico. A few kilometers from San Cristobal."

Frowning her confusion, Erin followed him to the waiting Jeep. Mexico? What was in Mexico? she wondered. The mission, obviously, judging by his brisk determination to get the show on the road. She glanced around once more. The area was desolate. No houses, not even a gas station. She tried to calculate how long they'd been in the air, but couldn't since she wasn't sure what time they'd left the prison. Four or five hours, she supposed.

Logan had awakened her a few minutes before the pilot had started the descent. He'd suggested she have some coffee and use the facilities since they were in for a long ride when they hit the ground. Erin had obediently complied. The coffee had been to die for. If Logan had made it, he was a true master. Sweet rolls had also been available, but Erin had opted not to start the day off with a sugar rush. Then again, she eyed the alien surroundings once more, maybe she should have. She climbed into the back seat of the Jeep and suddenly felt utterly empty. But she was pretty sure the emptiness had more to do with anxiety than hunger.

She was in deep trouble here. Was her freedom really worth coming to a foreign country to help in an unknown capacity on a *very* dangerous secret mission? She remembered quite clearly, he'd said *very* dangerous. What if these guys weren't even government agents? What if the credentials were fakes? Fear mushroomed inside her, making her chest tight. Why hadn't she thought of that before?

Well, it was a little late to be considering turning back now. Logan had said that once she boarded that plane there was no going back. Though she'd known him less than twenty-four hours, she had the distinct impression he didn't say anything he didn't mean.

Her heart thudded harder, sending a new rush of adrenaline through her. Running wasn't an option. She surveyed the desolate area once more. They'd catch her easily and even if by some stroke of luck they didn't, she'd never survive long enough to find her way to civilization. Camping skills had never been her strong suit. Her sense of direction was nonexistent and she didn't have a clue how to locate water in the desert or how to ignite a fire by rubbing sticks together. She was a city girl through and through.

The man who'd driven the SUV swung behind the wheel of the Jeep. "Here we go, then," he offered in a tone far too chipper for the occasion. Erin saw no levity whatsoever in the situation. She was likely going to die very soon and there was nothing she could do about it since she was still a prisoner with no rights—and these two men were her new guards.

Logan slid a pair of expensive-looking sunglasses into place and said something to the driver that she couldn't quite hear over the noisy engine. The driver nodded and pressed a little harder on the accelerator. Clutching the seat to keep from bouncing out of the vehicle, Erin studied John Logan for the first time. She'd been too shocked when they initially met at the prison to give him more than a cursory once-over, then it had been dark in the SUV on the way to the airport. Promptly falling asleep in flight had been nice, but had left her no time to consider the man who now basically owned her soul.

He was handsome. She'd noticed that before. Morning stubble further darkened his chiseled jaw, adding to his aura of danger. His skin was deeply tanned. She wondered if he spent most of his time in this type of climate. With his shirt sleeves rolled up she could see well-muscled forearms indicating strength. He was tall. She'd guess in the neighborhood of six-one or -two. Lean frame. He didn't say a lot, at least not to her. But when he did speak his voice was deep, resonate. Commanding, yet not harsh.

His hair was cut in one of those short styles where it swept up and back nicely without any help from designer mousse or styling gel. He had good hair. Silky, but full-bodied. She inclined her head for a better view of his broad shoulders. Wide and strong. Dependable yet—

He looked directly at her as if she'd spoken her

thoughts aloud. Startled, she sucked in a harsh breath. He couldn't have heard her, but he removed his shades and glanced down at her chest as if he had. His gaze lingered there, making her pulse react, before moving slowly back up to her face.

"Is there something on your mind, Bailey?"

She shook her head, then shouted over the wind and engine noise, "I'm fine."

He stared at her for two beats longer before turning away. Erin closed her eyes then and released the breath she'd been holding. She would be stronger than this. No way could she let his every word and every look rattle her. She had to be ready for whatever this mission required of her. This was her only chance to get her life back. No matter how dangerous, she had to make it.

Going back to that prison was not an option.

"WHAT IS THIS PLACE?" Erin asked, her voice sounding oddly loud after the two-hour trip with nothing but the grind and growl of the Jeep's engine.

The driver had parked the Jeep outside what looked like an ancient city, then disappeared inside its walls. Erin lifted an eyebrow in skepticism as she scanned the crumbling buildings once more. Ruins would be a more apt description than city. Her history and geography were a little rusty, but she recognized the architecture was far from contemporary in any sense of the word.

"Let's go, Bailey."

Startled, she looked around to find Logan waiting

outside the Jeep for her. He offered his hand. Still stunned or maybe numb, she accepted, allowing him to help her down from the vehicle. His hand felt warm around hers. Warm and steady. Something she needed desperately at the moment.

"What is this place?" she asked again, her curiosity definitely piqued.

"For the next six days it's home," he told her without actually telling her anything at all.

When he would have started forward, she snagged him by the arm. His skin felt hot beneath her fingers. She quickly jerked her hand back and flexed her tingling fingers, struggling to remember what she'd intended to say.

"What now?" he groused, frowning down at her from behind those infernal glasses.

She dragged her gaze back to the village before them. That was it. The place looked like an ancient village fallen upon hard times, deserted by its people. "How did you find this place?" She looked back up at him for the good it did with those dark lenses shielding his eyes. "Is this where the mission takes place?" She shook her head then. "None of this makes any sense. I don't understand." She gestured vaguely to the village. "What does this have to do with national security?"

He removed the glasses, tucked them into his shirt pocket and leveled that dark as midnight gaze on her. "This is our temporary training post." He nodded in the direction of the throng of mud huts and rustic stucco buildings. "The governor of Chiapas lent it to us because he owed my deputy director a favor. We have everything we need here. Now come on." He urged her forward. "I'll give you the grand tour. Then we'll eat." He glanced down at her, his eyebrow arched in clear skepticism this time. "You're going to need your strength. Lesson one starts this afternoon."

Erin followed Logan into what looked like a deserted building. A command post had been set up in the dilapidated chapel in the center of the village. Satellite communications—as well as older, less technically advanced radio-transmission systems—were in place. Two computers were up and running, linked to the Net. A massive generator provided the needed power.

There was what Logan called a mess hall and a physical training room. The bathing facilities weren't glamorous, but they had hot running water, soap and shampoo. What more could a girl on a dangerous mission ask for? Might as well look on the bright side, she told herself, rallying her make-the-best-of-it spirit.

Six of the smaller buildings had been prepared for lodging, Logan explained as they approached the first one of the group. "This one," he told her, "is yours." Then he pointed to the hut directly in front of hers. "I'll be there."

She poked her head inside the room he'd indicated as hers and was pleasantly surprised by the small but comfortable-looking cot. "It's better than I expected," she admitted as she turned back to him. "I was certain there'd be a sleeping bag on the ground in there." She tried for a smile, but didn't quite make it. She was just too tired and this was all far too overwhelming to work up enough enthusiasm no matter how hard she wanted to.

But it's real, she kept telling herself. And she was free. That's all that mattered, right?

Erin glanced around at the dozen or so armed men moving about. Well, maybe free wasn't precisely the right word.

"After I've evaluated your strengths and weaknesses, we'll move on to the finer details you'll need for this mission."

Here she was, way down in Mexico, right next to Guatemala if memory served her correctly, and she hadn't a clue why she was here. "Can you tell me more about the mission?" A girl could ask, she mused.

"This way, Bailey," he offered in reply, smoothly changing the course of the conversation, as well as her little sight-seeing tour.

The next building they entered was one of the largest and very dimly lit. An oily smell she couldn't readily identify hit her nostrils with the first breath she took. She squinted to better make out the boxes stacked around the room. Crates, she realized, wooden crates. Logan paused at the first one of three she counted. She peered inside. Instinctively she drew back at what she saw.

Guns. Lots of guns.

"M9 Personal Defense Weapon," Logan announced as he displayed one of the mean-looking guns from the crate. "Weapon of choice in personal defense."

"M4 Carbine," he went on, putting the first one aside and reaching for another, seemingly oblivious to her appalled expression. "Lightweight, magazine fed, selective rate, shoulder fired weapon. Even in tight quarters, a target can be engaged at extended range with accurate, lethal fire. Every terrorist's wet dream."

"Wait!" Erin backed away another step, her heart beginning to hammer. "I don't understand. Why are you telling me about these weapons?"

Tears welled unbidden. This was insane and what was worse she was going to cry. She hated crying. It made her feel weak. "I don't know anything about guns or terrorists or even personal defense." She lengthened the distance between them by another step, blinking furiously to hold back the infuriating tears. "Just tell me the truth, Logan. What am I doing here?" She flung her arm toward the weapons he appeared to gloat over. "What is all this?"

His glare was as lethal as the weapon he held in those strong, too capable hands. "This," he ground out, "is just a taste of what you need to know." He put down the weapon and started in her direction. She wanted to run, but froze instead. Those dark, dark eyes held her in a kind of trance. "You have six days, Bailey. Six days to learn what I have to teach you. And this is only scratching the surface. Then we go in, ready or not."

She trembled. "What if…what if I can't do it?" She couldn't. She was suddenly as sure of it as she'd ever been of anything in her whole life. This was impossible. She couldn't do this. Not for freedom, not for vengeance, not for anything.

Logan stopped mere inches from her, staring down at her with a face wiped clean of emotion. Her pulse thundered with the fear exploding inside her.

"Then you have six days to live," he said quietly, so damned quietly she wanted to scream. "Because on the seventh, we'll both be dead."

Chapter Three

She'd slowed down considerably. Logan resisted the urge to slow his own pace. She had to keep up or at least attempt to. Even if he had the luxury of time, which he didn't, there was no place in any of this for misguided sympathies or regrets. She'd signed on to do this despite the numerous opportunities he'd given her to change her mind, opportunities he'd had no authority to give. But he'd needed to be sure.

For five days now he had pushed Erin Bailey hard. She'd held up far better than he'd expected, but it was catching up to her now. Again he forced away the need to look over his shoulder and check on her. Five days and he still hadn't concluded his evaluation, was far from certain about anything. Sure, she managed to scrape by physically. She'd obviously been a runner before checking into Atlanta's premiere federal resort. But holding up physically wouldn't be enough. She had to be able to take the mental pressure.

He clenched his jaw and commanded his body to move forward, his long legs eating up the ground beneath him as his second wind kicked in, sending endorphins rushing through his veins. The hot desert sand sucked at his running shoes while the scorching morning sun milked the sweat from him, but he ignored both. He banished images of Erin Bailey's struggle to keep up. She spent entirely too much unnecessary time in his head lately. He didn't want to think about her as a person…only her ability to perform as his partner and the mission.

The mission…nothing else mattered.

"I can't go any farther."

Logan wanted desperately to disregard the feeble cry that came from some ten meters behind him. He wanted this mission over, wanted to pretend that certain death wasn't lurking a mere forty-eight hours away. He slowed to a stop, braced his hands on his hips and took a moment to catch his breath, to compose himself really, before double-timing it back to where Bailey had stalled. She was bent over at the waist, her palms resting on her knees for support. He didn't have to look to know that her arms and legs would be quivering with weakness. He'd pushed her harder today than the last two put together.

"Suck it up, *partner*, it's five miles back to camp." He swiped away the sweat rolling down his forehead. "We don't have all day."

She dropped to her knees in the sand, then stared up at him, squinting against the sun at his back. "I said—" she gasped for breath between each word "—I have to rest."

He shifted just enough to allow the sun to beat down more fully on her. Her right hand automatically went up to shield her face. "While you're resting," he suggested, obviously going soft since he didn't have it in him to drag her to her feet, "tell me about yourself."

A few seconds passed before she responded. In that time Logan noted far more than he wanted to. Her blond hair, though pulled back in a ponytail, was mussed and slipping loose now. Long, silky wisps clung to the damp skin of her neck. Her face was flushed with exhaustion. Heavy-duty sunscreen was all that kept her delicate complexion from burning beneath the sun's savagery. The rapid rise and fall of her chest stole his attention momentarily and before he could stop it. Her sweat-soaked T-shirt clung to her, outlining her breasts and disrupting his own heart rate.

"My name is Sara Wilks." She scrubbed both hands over her face, then dropped them to her knees and pushed to her feet. She took a moment to regain her equilibrium and Logan resisted the urge to reach out and steady her.

She frowned petulantly. "But you call me Baby."

She didn't like his pet name for her, but it was the easiest way to go considering he didn't have time for her to get used to Sara. He'd called Jess "Baby" often enough in front of the right people for it to work. Both he and Jess had taken variations on their own names for their cover. As far as Esteban was concerned, he was Logan Wilks and Jess was his wife Sara.

"I'm twenty-five," she continued, then sucked in a desperate breath. "And I'm from Atl—"

He bit back the curse that sprang to the tip of his tongue. "You're from where?" he demanded sharply.

"Austin," she spat, shading her eyes once more so that she could glare at him. "Austin, Texas. I like guns...any kind. And if you mess with me, I'll kill you."

She said the last with a little more conviction than usual. Logan had the distinct impression that she meant it. "How long have we been together?" He started to walk, turning back to see that she followed.

"Three years." She smiled saccharinely before starting forward. "My momma warned me about guys like you, but I didn't listen. I just wanted out of Texas."

Logan grinned. That was new. He liked it. "What about guys like me?" he prodded as he eased into a jog.

"You lie. You cheat. You steal." She fell into stride next to him. "You do whatever necessary to get the job done. You're former military. Got busted for drugs and went AWOL before you were court-martialed. You've killed five men, two for looking at me the wrong way."

So far so good. Just the one slip. He was impressed. She was doing much better today than yesterday. "What was our last job?"

"We smuggled some weapons from Canada to a militia group in Montana." She shot him a sideways glance. "Almost got caught, too, because you pissed off one of the guys with the buyer."

"Very good." Logan picked up the pace, she did the same. "And the one before that."

"Drug smuggling. The Mexican authorities are still looking for us."

"Then maybe we'd better get back to camp before they catch us out here in the open," he said nonchalantly.

Her eyes went wide for the space of one beat, then she shot him a drop-dead look before breaking into a full-fledged sprint. About time she got her second wind, Logan mused as he surged forward, easily catching up with her.

Yep, she was determined. That much was certain. She could hold her own physically. It was the fright factor that had him worried. There was only one way to measure her ability to cope with that part. He forced away a prick of regret. He had no choice. Erin Bailey's life, as well as his own, depended upon her reactions.

He had to know what they would be.

And time was running out.

"Good God, Bailey, you're dead already. In a real time situation, a miss gives your target an opportunity to return fire."

Erin tossed her weapon onto the sand and stomped toward Logan. "That's it." She glared at him. Her pulse reacted instantly. God, she hated that. All week she'd been fighting this insane little physical attraction to the big jerk. "I'm calling it a day." It was almost dark after all and she was beat. They'd been at this since before dawn. She couldn't think, much less get a bead on a target.

"And nothing you can say will change my mind."

She stopped right in front of him and dared him to argue.

She should have known better.

Those dark eyes fairly glittered with annoyance. "Pick up your weapon, Bailey."

It wasn't as much his ruthless tone as it was the expression on that handsome face: He was madder than hell. The reality gave Erin pause, but she didn't budge.

"Now," he added in a lethal growl.

Her jaw clenched, Erin spun away from him. "Jerk," she muttered as she strode back to the abandoned weapon. A few other choice expletives flashed through her mind as she retrieved the black 9 mm weapon. What the hell had she been thinking agreeing to this crazy scheme? Clearly Jeff's betrayal and her subsequent time in prison had affected her more profoundly than she'd realized. She whipped back toward her overbearing mentor prepared to demand what he wanted her to do now and found herself face to chest with him.

"Take aim at that target like you *want* to hit it," he ordered curtly.

She wanted to hit something all right, but it wasn't the human silhouette hanging on the other side of the makeshift firing range. Still, she did as she was told since she couldn't be completely sure of what he'd do if she didn't. She braced her left hand beneath her right wrist and closed one eye to peer down the barrel.

"Feet shoulder width apart."

The sharply snapped command came at the same

instant that a strong arm wrapped around her waist and hauled her against a hard male physique. Her breath caught. With her body held firmly against him, Logan kicked her feet apart.

"Now, fire," he ordered.

She obeyed. Her arm flew up with the recoil. The shot went to the right of the target.

Logan swore under his breath. One powerful arm still pinning her waist, he reached out with the other and held her arm steady. "Take your time, Bailey," he said, his mouth close to her ear. Too close. She could feel his warm breath on the sensitive skin there. "Focus. Hitting that target could mean the difference between life and death. You do want to live, don't you, *Baby?*"

"Yes," she hissed.

She hated it when he called her that, but, at the moment, very distracting sensations were bombarding her, eliminating any possibility of a clever rebuttal. The feel of him, hard, undeniably male, pressed against her buttocks, along the backs of her thighs. His arm around her, fingers splayed just beneath her breast. Oh, and the heady scent—male sweat mixed with his own unique musky smell... Seven long months of abstinence were finally taking their toll.

"Focus," he murmured thickly.

Erin frowned. Was it her imagination, or was he holding her even more tightly now? Before she could sort through the new awareness generated by his unexpected reaction, he ordered, "Fire!"

She obeyed.

And missed yet again.

He muttered a stinging curse.

"You have to focus, Bailey!" He released her and stormed a few feet away as if needing the distance. He glared first at her, then at the unmarred silhouette.

She struggled to steady herself after the abrupt absence of his body against hers. A whole new barrage of sensations flooded her now. Need, sharp and demanding. And desire, dammit. Desire and disappointment. Disappointment at no longer having him near...for failing to please him.

God, she had lost whatever mind she had left.

He turned toward her then, the savage look on his face sending her stumbling back a couple of steps. "Forty-eight hours, Bailey." He moved closer. "*Two days.* That's all we have left. You've got to try harder."

She shook her head in protest of his accusation. "I'm doing the best I can."

"You have to do better." He stopped directly in front of her and stared down at her with a fierceness that undid the last of her bravado. "Tell me about the weapon you seem to be having so much trouble using."

She hesitated.

Logan cursed himself for the fool he was.

How could Lucas think for one minute that he could do this? There was no way she would be ready. Physical endurance wasn't nearly enough.

"The weapon, *Baby,*" he snapped. "Tell me about the weapon you're holding."

"Don't call me that," she shouted back, sounding tired and disgusted.

He inclined his head and glared at her. "Get used to it. Now tell me about the weapon."

Distress instantly replaced any anger she'd shown. Bailey stared at the gun in her hand as if it could somehow answer for her. "It's a 9 mm...ah..." She shook her head and lifted her gaze back to his. "I can't remember what kind."

Those huge violet eyes shimmered with uncertainty and no small amount of fear. He swore again, silently this time. He had to find a way to tap into her anger. When she was angry she tried harder, fought back.

"Then tell me about mine." He held the weapon up where she could see it. "I gave you a block of instruction on both a few hours ago."

She chewed her lower lip, giving away her every emotion. Jess would never have done that.

"Forty cal Glock," he barked impatiently as he showed her both sides of the weapon. "Weapon of choice these days by most federal agencies. Similar in weight and size to the 9 mm, but with more deadly force. *Combat Tupperware.*"

She shook her head, defeat sagging her shoulders. "I hate guns," she admitted. "I don't want to know anything about them."

Fury charged through him. He snagged her right hand, drawing the weapon up where she had no choice but to look at it. He was out of time. He had to know now if she could take the heat. It was the only way. He hated the idea of putting her through what was to come…except his options were sorely limited. He'd come to that conclusion last night and had made the necessary arrangements for their next adventure.

"This is a Beretta," he explained. "Very popular. Light weight, efficient." He tightened his fingers around hers. "This weapon could save your life."

She shook her head again, tears brimming this time. Just what he needed. "I can't do this. You've got the wrong girl for the job."

He let go of her hand. "You have to do it. And you're the *only* girl for the job."

"You might as well take me back to Atlanta." Her fearful gaze collided with his. "I could never shoot anyone." She closed her eyes and drew in a ragged breath. "I just can't do it, Logan. Face it. This isn't going to work."

Wrong answer. They'd come too far to back out now. He wouldn't let her give up just yet. "When you have an extreme situation, Bailey, you have to take extreme measures. Remember that."

Before she could fathom his intent, he'd pressed the barrel of his Glock against her forehead. Disbelief registered on her face. "What're you doing?"

"The question is what're you going to do, Bailey? You've got a gun pointed directly at your head. You have to do something."

"This is crazy. You've—"

"Do something, Bailey! If you hesitate, you're dead."

"Wait!"

"I dragged you into this messy situation. I've been

pushing you day and night. Fight back! Do something!''

''I…I can't do what you need me to do.''

''Then you'll die.'' A definite *click* echoed around them as he cocked his weapon. ''Do something, Bailey. Do it now!''

That deer-in-the-headlights look captured her expression as the color drained from her face. She lifted the Beretta, jabbed it toward him as if that alone were a monumental effort.

''It's going to take more than that. Shoot,'' he commanded, ''or I will.''

She trembled. Once. Twice. Her spine stiffened. ''You're bluffing,'' she challenged, a glimmer of courage peeking past the fear in her eyes.

''Do you really want to take that chance? What exactly do you know about me? Are you sure you can trust me? I could kill you and who would know?'' He leaned forward, putting himself nose-to-nose with her. ''Who would care?''

Fury tightened her lips.

About time.

He pressed the barrel a little harder against her. ''Who's going first, *Baby*, you or me?''

He saw the subtle change in her eyes a fraction of a second before the resounding *snap* of the Beretta's empty chamber announced that she had, indeed, depressed the trigger.

A smile slid across his face as surprise, then confusion and fear claimed her features. And here he'd worried she didn't have it in her. "Very good, Bailey."

The spent weapon fell from her limp fingers. "You son of a bitch." The luster of fear disappeared from her eyes and was quickly replaced by glittering anger. "You knew it was empty. You goaded me into—" She moved in the last remaining inches between them and glared up at him. "You knew it was empty and you put me through that!"

Right on both counts. He'd known she'd used her last round *and* he'd worn a vest. He never went on a firing range with a newbie without sporting Kevlar. He hadn't lived this long by being stupid. "At least we know now that you can shoot a man if you have to."

In a metamorphosis that surprised him, she reared back and shoved hard at his chest with both hands, unbalancing him momentarily. "You are a jerk, Logan! And I've had enough!" Her eyes flared with fury. "Cut the cloak-and-dagger crap and tell me what's going on! Why am I here?"

This was much more like it. He'd been waiting for her to demand some answers, had about decided it wasn't going to happen. Damned if the woman wasn't full of surprises.

"All right." He tucked his weapon back into the waistband of his jeans. "Pablo Esteban is the most powerful man alive in the cocaine trade. Everybody from the CIA to DEA wants him…has tried to nail him, but he's too clever. He never makes a mistake.

Never leaves Colombia. Never gets caught in a compromising position."

Logan erased a new line of sweat from his brow with his forearm, then rested his hands on his hips. "About a year ago he branched out into the arms trade. Now he steals military weapons and sells them to the lowlife around the globe. We're going to stop him, but first we have to find out who's leaking him the info on where and when to find the weapons."

Glistening with perspiration, Bailey's skin took on a definite greenish quality as she absorbed all that he said. Though still clearly angry, she looked on the verge of tossing her lunch. "Oh, God."

Obviously what he'd told her was far more than she'd bargained for.

"How can we stop him?" she asked wanly.

"We'll get to that," Logan assured her. That was enough information for her to assimilate at the moment. "For now, just be glad you can do what you have to if the need arises." He chucked her on the shoulder. "Surely if you can shoot me, you can shoot the bad guys."

The reality of what she'd done seemed to hit her full force all over again. Her stance wilted. Any lingering anger dissolved, leaving those big eyes suspiciously bright. "I didn't mean to...I just..."

He picked up her weapon, popped in a fresh clip. "Defended yourself," he finished for her. "That's a start."

"Oh my..." Her hand flew to her mouth. Fainting appeared a distinct possibility.

"Sit. Put your head between your knees," he ordered.

The sound of engines roaring in the distance drew Logan's attention to the west. Phase two was about to begin. If she passed out now that would screw up everything.

"Who's that?"

His gaze locked with hers. "Run!"

She stiffened, instantly alert. "What is it?"

He refused to acknowledge the renewed fear in her eyes. "Looks like the governor double-crossed me."

She frowned, confusion overriding her fear for the moment. "What?"

He thrust the Beretta at her. "Remember, we're wanted drug smugglers in this country. Run, dammit!"

As if in slow motion, Erin turned in the direction of the approaching sound. Three Jeeps were speeding toward them. The men inside the vehicles all wore khaki uniforms. It took another couple of seconds for her mind to wrap around the realization that it was the authorities.

Logan tugged her forward.

How far away was the camp? Two miles? They'd never make it. The Jeep they'd arrived in was more than a hundred yards away. They wouldn't even make it that far.

A cloud of dust swept over them. Engines roaring, the vehicles surrounded them. Erin's heart pounded harder. Logan suddenly skidded to a stop and pulled her behind him. Her mind raced with the possibilities, all too horrible to say out loud.

This couldn't be happening.

Blackness threatened her for the second time today. She sucked in a ragged breath and fought to stay vertical and alert. Voices echoed. Logan moved in a circle, keeping her behind him as he faced the threat.

When the dust settled, more than a dozen weapons were trained on them. Erin clutched Logan's shirt. What could they do? Nothing. They couldn't possibly fight this many men.

"Remember everything I taught you, Bailey," Logan muttered over his shoulder.

"Caiga sus armas!"

Erin jerked at the harsh order for them to drop their weapons.

It was over.

They were dead and it wasn't even the seventh day.

SHE WAS STILL ALIVE.

That in itself felt like a miracle.

Erin paced the primitive cell. It was larger than the one she'd called home back in Atlanta, but lacked the modern conveniences. She glanced at what passed for a toilet and sink and grimaced. Well, at least she was alive.

She stalled in the middle of her dingy surroundings and prayed the same was true of Logan. The police had separated them as soon as they arrived at the prison camp. She'd been practically strip-searched. Thank God she'd been allowed to keep on her underwear. She closed her eyes and fought the urge to cry. Unlike in the United States, there had been no female chaperone during the proceedings. Once the guard had given her a thorough once-over, he'd told her to get dressed.

The interrogation had begun then. They'd questioned her for over two hours. Erin hugged her arms around herself and tried to ease the weak but steady trembling rampant in her. She'd managed to stick to her story. She was Sara Wilks from Austin. They'd shown her a wanted poster with a picture of Logan and his former partner. The mirror image of herself, only with black hair, had stared back at Erin. The likeness was eerie. The man who appeared to be in charge had questioned her unmercifully. Called her a liar on more than one occasion and suggested that perhaps she needed additional motivation to tell the truth. She'd known what he meant. She fully expected to be dragged from the cell any time now and tortured until she said what they wanted to hear.

Erin threaded her fingers through her hair and released a heavy breath. Maybe she should just tell them the truth about who she was and where she'd actually come from. But Logan had warned her to remember everything he'd taught her. There had to be some reason he didn't want these people to know the truth. She paced the length of the cell again. Would they kill them if they knew the truth or would it simply blow their cover for the mission?

She frowned, confusion and renewed fear drilling into her brain. Logan was too smart to let anything like this happen, wasn't he? A man with enough clout to come into a federal prison in the middle of the night and leave with a prisoner surely knew his business.

But here they were just the same. In a Mexican prison that verified everything she'd ever heard about the less than savory institutions.

She remembered enough Spanish from high school to understand that they were in deep trouble. Obviously believing that she didn't comprehend a word they said, the men had spoken freely. She shuddered when she recalled the remarks one had made about what he would like to do to her.

Footsteps coming from somewhere beyond her line of vision jerked her attention to the bars at the front of the cell. Her chest tightened with renewed dread. Logan, flanked by two guards, stopped at the door. Her heart did a funny little leap at the sight of him. She resisted the urge to shake her head. It just wouldn't do to analyze that bit of irony. She was stuck in this place because of Logan and yet she couldn't stop such a silly reaction to him. Thankfully, he looked no worse for the wear. She'd imagined all sorts of terrible things the guards might have done to him. She shuddered when she considered some of the ones she'd feared would be done to her before this was over.

Prayer appeared to be their only recourse now. If their circumstances grew any more dire, that might not even help.

"Abra la célula y déjenos."

The order to unlock her cell and leave them came

from Logan. Stunned, Erin watched in disbelief as the two guards obeyed without hesitation.

Silence thickened for a full minute before she could bring herself to do anything other than stare at Logan. The woman in her reveled in every handsome detail of his face and his tall, lean frame. And at the same time, her more rational side demanded that she fear this man she scarcely knew and who had complete power over her universe. The most ludicrous part was that somehow, some part of her trusted him though she knew she shouldn't.

"I don't understand," she finally managed to articulate. None of this made sense. Had Logan somehow talked his way out of this predicament? Were they free to go now? Was the mission blown?

"You did good, Bailey," he said, a wide grin spreading across his beard-shadowed face. "I didn't think you had it in you, but you did."

The epiphany dawned three seconds later. "This was a setup." The anger she'd felt when he forced her to fire that weapon at him when she hadn't wanted to slammed into her twofold.

"A test," he countered. "We had to be sure you could take the mental pressure." He leaned against the open door. "This was the only way to gauge it."

"I thought they were going to kill me." She advanced on him. He'd let her think the worst. Let her waste her time and energy worrying about him... praying for him. "I worried that you were being tortured or worse." She poked him in the chest with her forefinger. "And all the while you were probably sitting at some desk with your feet up and laughing your ass off at how gullible I am.''

He folded his arms over his chest, for protection maybe because she definitely had murder on her mind. ''Actually I've been observing your reaction to interrogation.'' He cocked an eyebrow. ''I am impressed, Bailey. You stuck with the story until the bitter end.''

Erin could barely hear him over the roar of fury in her ears. She struggled to keep her cool, but it was becoming increasingly difficult with him looking so damned smug about the whole thing.

''I'm surprised you didn't go for three or four hours!'' she fairly shouted, her cool disappearing completely in spite of her best efforts. ''How can you be sure two hours of interrogation was enough? Maybe my humiliation wasn't quite complete.''

His gaze turned dead serious. ''Because any more than that would have been a waste. Esteban doesn't waste time. He would either have believed you by then or he would have killed you.''

She held that too serious gaze for a couple of anxious seconds more before another blast of fury shored up her waning anger. ''No more surprises, Logan.'' She planted her hands on her hips and glared at him. His only reaction was another of those infuriating grins. ''I mean it. If I'm in this thing, I'm in all the way. You keep me up to speed on what's going on or I'm out. Do you hear me? *No…more…surprises.*''

''Loud and clear, Bailey.'' He straightened and stared down at her. ''There's just one more thing we have to get out of the way first.''

She braced herself for yet another tactical maneuver. The sudden realization that he'd seen her in her underwear during the body search seared through her brain. "I'd better get advance warning from now on before you say or do anything," she cautioned. No way was she playing this game one minute longer.

"Agreed."

Uh-oh. That was entirely too easy.

"Today's our third anniversary, Baby."

She hated that he called her that. But that's what Logan Wilks, aka John Logan, had deemed the best solution for ensuring she didn't forget who she was. It was part of the cover. But she didn't have to like it.

"So," she shot back. "What's that got to do with here and now? And I don't want you calling me Baby unless it's necessary."

"Everything I do is necessary," he told her in a tone that brooked no argument. "And our anniversary is the reason we were able to put off joining Esteban a week ago. He thinks we've been in the Bahamas having a second honeymoon. In just over twenty-four hours, he's going to be expecting to see a couple fresh from a week of sharing 'Kodak' moments."

"Get to the point, Logan," she demanded, impatient. "What is it you have to get out of the way before we can ditch this dump?"

She should have seen it coming. Should have at least suspected, but she hadn't.

Logan kissed her. Took her face in his hands,

plunged his fingers into her hair and held her there while his mouth plundered hers.

She struggled at first, but the feel of his firm lips on hers soon turned coaxing. She flattened her palms against his chest in a last-ditch effort to shove him away, but failed miserably. Instead, her fingers immediately fisted in the cotton of his shirt, effectively drawing him nearer when she should have pushed him away.

Fire rushed through her veins, heating her skin, heightening the desire that had been there, way deep down, from the start. Something had clicked for her the moment she laid eyes on him. A regard that, despite the external wariness between them, only deepened with time and proximity.

He eased closer to her, aligning himself more fully with her, allowing the subtlest contact. His tongue traced her lips and she opened for him, took him inside her. Her feminine muscles reacted, tightened. Her heart thundered beneath her sternum. The idea that the guards might be watching didn't matter. Her entire being was consumed with the taste of him…the feel of his mouth on hers…the hunger of her body for his. She melted against him, molding fully to his incredibly male frame. If he stripped her naked and took her right there against the crumbling cell wall, she wouldn't have tried to stop him. His touch was magic, his taste drugging. She was his for the taking.

He drew back, his uneven breath fanning her sizzling lips. Then he released her and stepped away.

The haze of lust cleared from his expression instantly. "I needed to be sure you could be convincing as my loving wife and not bolt and run."

She went rigid. Another test. Not real. Just a test. The blood rushed to her face, staining her cheeks. It had been all too real for her, but he didn't have to know that. "Save the theatrics for an audience, Logan," she retorted. "You're not the first man I've kissed and you won't be the last."

One corner of his mouth twitched, infuriating her all the more. "I didn't think I would be." He hitched his thumb toward the exit. "Let's get going. We have final preparations to make before heading to Colombia."

She grabbed him by the arm before he could get away. "We're going to Colombia now?" Her heart was racing again. No more tests. This would be the real thing. Life and death. There couldn't be any wrong moves.

"That's right, Bailey. We leave tomorrow night. By dawn the day after that, we'll be in Esteban's compound." That dark, dark gaze searched hers. "Are you ready to risk your life for me, *Baby?*"

Erin steeled herself against the deluge of emotions that threatened to rain down upon her. She was past the point of no return already. There was no other choice. She wanted her freedom back—wanted her life back. *This was for her.*

"Yeah," she returned pointedly. "I'm ready to risk my life for *me.*"

A slow smile slid across his handsome face and something electrical passed between them...a connection or an interest of sorts, only it went far deeper than the physical. His gaze held hers until the moment passed.

"Let's do it then."

Erin followed him down the dank corridor. She said one final prayer for their safety as the events of the past six days whirled through her mind. She could do things she'd never dreamed herself capable of. She was stronger than she'd known, but would it be enough to keep her alive?

Would it be enough, she admitted, to keep Logan alive?

Chapter Four

Erin's first look at the country of Colombia was breathtaking. The jagged lines of the Andes Mountains, covered with emerald green trees, jutted heavenward and were draped in low-lying clouds. The glimpse of a major city nestled amid the soaring peaks gave the impression of vulnerability. But Erin knew from Logan's description that the city of Medellín was anything but vulnerable. It was a place where evil lurked behind seemingly innocuous, everyday facades. A place where no one was safe from the cartel's far-reaching iron grip. Though certainly not every citizen of the vast city was a part of the cartel, anyone who resided there had likely been touched in one way or another by the insidious presence of one drug lord or another.

There was no real escape.

What a fitting destination.

Erin looked away. How could her life have come to this? She was a quiet, passive individual. She'd never purposely harmed anyone. The idea that she was now a criminal—a prisoner—still startled her. She'd grown up in a small town a few miles west of Atlanta. An only child, her parents had doted on her constantly. She'd been their whole world, as they had been hers. Then one day her mother didn't show up after school. Erin had waited and waited, but no one came. Just before dark a patrol car had arrived and taken her to the local police station. Her parents had died in a car crash that afternoon.

In an instant, her whole world changed.

Erin blinked back the tears that never failed to accompany thoughts of her parents. She'd had no other family, but couldn't complain about the foster home the system had chosen for her. The Martins had been good to her, but she had never allowed herself to love them or trust them completely. She hadn't meant to hold back her emotions, it just happened.

Some part of her had simply closed down after the loss of her parents. She'd only been twelve after all. Her heart wouldn't let her trust anyone again the way she'd trusted her parents. They were supposed to be there for her and one day they were suddenly gone. As an adult she understood that it certainly wasn't by choice or by any fault of theirs, but the lonely, heart-broken child in her couldn't forgive them for leaving her. She'd loved them so much. It wasn't until Jeff that she'd permitted herself to feel that emotion again.

And look where it had gotten her. He had assured her that what she was doing was legal, that he had the various companies' permission for her to attempt to breach their cyber security. What a liar he'd been. Oh, he'd proven his company's worth all right, but she had paid the price.

No way would she ever trust anyone with her heart again.

Erin forced the emotion from her eyes and focused her attention to the here and now. The same plane that had flown them from Atlanta to Mexico touched down at a rustic, out-of-the-way airfield a few miles from their intended final destination.

The landing wasn't smooth. She braced herself and hoped the pilot knew how to stop this thing before they ran out of landing strip. Her knuckles whitened where she gripped the armrests as the plane hurtled toward a wall of dense woods...the same ones she'd admired only moments ago. The breath stalled in her lungs as the screech of straining brakes and engines shattered the quiet.

The plane skidded to a stop just yards shy of plunging into the tree line. Several seconds elapsed before Erin remembered to breathe. Some part of her kept expecting the crash, but it never came. Fear dropped to a more tolerable level, and her focus slowly widened to include the others onboard the aircraft.

"Up and at 'em, Bailey," Logan said as he stood. "This is where the fun begins."

He flashed her that too cocky grin of his as Erin fumbled with her safety belt, released it then pushed out of her seat. He never smiled except for that cocksure twisting of his lips. She'd figured out his motivation for the flirtatious and completely unnerving gesture. He knew it rattled her and that was his goal.

Most times when she got rattled, she got mad. He wanted her angry. At the moment, she wished it was that simple. Anger had taken a back seat—way back— to the terror climbing up her spine. She felt numbed by it, but squared her shoulders and bit back the fear she didn't want him to see.

Her attempt crashed and burned.

Logan read her too easily. She saw the understanding in his eyes a fraction of a second before he blinked it away. "There's an SUV, a rental, waiting for us here. It was rented in Bogota yesterday, along with a hotel room, where a man and woman vaguely matching our descriptions stayed the night. We'll drive back to Medellín and then on to Esteban's compound from there."

When he started to turn away, Erin asked, "What was the name of the hotel?" She had to remember to pay attention, to be keenly observant. He'd told her that over and over. It was all about the mission now.

Logan looked back at her. "The Bogota Plaza." A hint of a real smile touched that usually controlled expression of his. "Very good, Bailey."

Erin relaxed marginally then. She'd finally done the impossible. She'd actually impressed John Logan outside one of his initiated tests. Wow. Maybe there was hope. Or maybe leaving out the name of the hotel *was* a test. Erin shook off the thought. She couldn't walk around worrying whether she'd met his expectations. They were on the same side.

The temperature felt considerably cooler outside than what they'd left behind at the makeshift training center. Erin chafed her arms and wished for the jacket that was in her duffel. The air was noticeably thinner as well. Logan had warned her about that and the headaches that might come before her body adjusted to the unfamiliar altitude.

Ramon, the driver, loaded Logan and Erin's duffels into the back of an SUV. Maverick, the pilot, was in deep, hushed conversation with Logan. Erin, as usual, was the outsider. Part of, but not quite in, the discussions and planning. She hated that arrangement. Logan still didn't let her all the way in. Not even after she'd passed all his little tests. She shivered as she considered the events of the past couple of days. Profound disbelief flooded her each time she recalled how Logan had goaded her into pulling that trigger with the weapon aimed directly at him.

What if he'd made a mistake and there had been one final round in her clip? Oh, he'd laughed and said that was what Kevlar was for. But still, Erin hadn't liked it. Couldn't believe he'd go to that kind of extreme measure.

He had made his point rightly enough. She'd had to face the reality that she was capable of far more than she would ever have believed. Maybe it was all the accumulated stress of the past few months, combined with the unprecedented pressure of the past week. Who knew? Whatever the case, Erin now conceded that she could do what she had to. She shuddered at the thought. What would her parents think of her now?

Then again…

A smile suddenly tugged the corners of her mouth

upward. Wouldn't Jeff think twice about double-crossing her now? She might not have been such an easy target if she'd shown half the strength in the past that she'd dredged up under Logan's tutelage. A new surge of determination solidified her shaky resolve. Logan had promised Jeff would get his if she helped with this mission. From now on that would be her battle cry, the dangling carrot to keep her going.

She would do whatever it took to see that justice was served. All she had to do was stay alive to see it.

Watch out, Jeffrey, old boy, I'm coming for you.

Bailey had a definite purpose about her stride this morning, Logan noted. The decision to leave her hair blond had been the right one, he acknowledged as well. Women dyed their hair frequently enough. Esteban wouldn't experience more than a moment's pause over that particular detail. Knowing the man's fetish for blondes, he'd probably like it. But that hadn't been the primary motivation for the decision.

Besides being a top-notch driver and crack shot, Ramon had been a hairdresser in a former life. In his expert opinion, capturing Jess's exact hair color without Bailey's hair turning out too black or too *salon-done* would be next to impossible. It was better for it to appear that she had decided to go blond than for anyone to notice that her supposedly natural color looked a little "unnatural."

In addition, Ramon had suggested that Bailey go for a more "voluptuous" look. To that end, he'd layered her hair and shown her how to tease and spike the straight tresses. With tight jeans and an equally tight top that displayed a couple of inches of her midriff, she looked the part Jess had played.

But she wasn't Jess.

Logan took a deep, cleansing breath. He had to keep that reality tightly compartmentalized until this was over. He and Jess had been a team for a long time, they'd been close. Grief nipped at his heels every minute of every day. But he had to stay focused, had to get this done. Jess would want it that way. He had to do it for her. And then he would make sure Sanchez got what was coming to him. No matter what Lucas and Casey said, Logan would personally see to it that the scumbag paid dearly.

Forcing his attention back to the present, Logan watched Bailey circle the SUV as if she wanted to memorize its every detail. A weary smile hitched his lips. She was a quick study, there was no denying that. And, he had to admit, her computer skills were just a degree more advanced than Jess's. Another admission he didn't like making. She'd cracked every secure fire-wall and security net he'd put before her in record time. Bailey was good. No wonder her ex's cyber se-curity business had taken off. With a Grade A "hacker" like her, no place was off-limits in the cyber world, and she knew just what to do to make a system safe because of it. As long as she didn't break under the pressure or say the wrong thing in Esteban's pres-ence, Logan was convinced she could get the job done.

But she was so damned far out of her element. Would she be able to remain composed when the bul-lets started flying around her? When people started dying around her? Or when Esteban went on one of his famous rampages? Would she be able to play this game all the way out—whatever it took—until they were clear?

Logan suppressed the concern that surged inside him each time he considered anything beyond the next five minutes. He'd told Lucas just last night during the final teleconference that he still had major concerns. But it was too late to back out now. He hadn't needed Lucas to tell him that. Logan knew it better than anyone involved.

"Hey, man, are you following me here?"

Logan jerked to attention, then frowned when he realized he'd lost all track of what Maverick was reporting to him. "Let's go back to yesterday's activities," Logan suggested as if he simply wanted to hear that part again. "When did the Caldarone brothers arrive at the compound?"

"At 1600," Maverick deadpanned, then shook his head slowly from side to side. "Don't try to fool me, Johnny boy," he warned knowingly. "I told Lucas you could handle this. I wasn't wrong, was I?"

Logan met the other man's scrutinizing gaze. "I don't need you or Lucas checking up on me. If I wasn't up to the challenge we wouldn't be here. You know me better than that."

About forty, Maverick had a military demeanor, which dared anyone to mess with him and a piercing glare that could undermine any man's confidence. But not Logan's. Maverick had trained Logan as a specialist. The man was too much like a brother to put any fear in Logan. Ramon and Maverick were part of Mission Recovery's Detail and Housekeeping team. They took care of the little things, like Bailey's hair and setting up the phony couple at the hotel and renting the SUV. And, when necessary, they cleaned up behind a field operative.

Maverick looked from Logan to Bailey and back. "She's not Jess. This whole damned thing hinges on your being able to keep her out of trouble. The only way you'll be able to do that is by keeping your head on straight about who Erin Bailey really is—"

"I know she's not Jess," Logan ground out, his impatience quickly whipping into fury.

"I've watched you two together, Johnny," Maverick said quietly, his tone tight yet carefully controlled. "There's something there. Any fool could see it." He raised a hand when Logan would have argued. "It's a good thing, to an extent. Esteban will see it, too. Use it to your advantage. It doesn't matter if it's based on plain old protective instincts or just basic sexual interest. Use it, but don't *lose* it. You hear what I'm saying, Johnny boy? Even the best has his Achilles' heel. Just maybe this woman, considering the circumstances that brought the two of you together, is yours."

"And maybe the altitude has gotten to you," Logan said as he met that steely gaze with lead in his own. "You should know by now that I've never let anything, certainly not a woman, stop me from accomplishing the mission."

Maverick didn't say anything for what felt like a

full minute, just studied Logan as if he needed to confirm that last statement. "Yeah." Maverick let go a bark of tension-releasing laughter, backing off physically and mentally. "You're right, Johnny boy, you always get the job done." He slapped Logan on the back as they started toward the waiting SUV. "I'd go through a door with you anytime, even with that frightened little filly over there in tow."

To his supreme irritation, Logan's gaze settled on the filly in question just as she nervously forked her fingers through her hair. She forced a smile at something Ramon said, as she clasped her arms over her chest. She was nervous all right—with good reason, Logan admitted. She was about to enter into an alien world where no one could be trusted and nothing was what it seemed.

This was as far as Maverick and Ramon would go. Logan and Bailey would be on their own from here. He wondered if she fully understood that once inside Esteban's compound, no one could help them. Maybe it was better that she didn't.

"Good luck, Logan." Ramon nodded to him, then winked at Bailey. "Don't let him bully you, honey. He may be the boss, but you're the key."

Erin didn't quite know how to respond. "Thanks for the advice."

"By the time we return to Chiapas, the training center will have been packed up and we'll be on our way back to the States," Maverick said to Logan. "Ferrelli is your G.A. for this one." He turned to Erin and instantly realized she didn't understand. "Guardian angel," he explained. "Ferrelli will watch your backs to the extent possible when you're outside the compound. Inside, be sure to keep your head low, Bailey."

She smiled as best she could, which may have turned out to be no more than a twitch. She'd done a lot of that this morning.

This was it. The reality closed in around her like the tightening of a noose around her neck as she watched Maverick and Ramon climb back into the plane. A few minutes later and they were airborne. She watched until they were out of sight, her heart racing, her mind paralyzed with the mounting fear.

The sound of a vehicle door opening dragged Erin's attention to the SUV. Logan waited by the open passenger side door.

"Time to go to work, *Baby*."

She blinked, then shivered. Not so much from the annoying way he said the word, but from the way that dark, dark gaze skimmed her body in punctuation of it. Steeling herself, Erin walked over to where he waited, but hesitated before climbing into the vehicle. She had to find a way to keep her balance with him…to even the playing field.

"Tell me, Logan," she said in the most seductive tone she could marshal. "Didn't Jess have a pet name for you?" She shrugged. "I mean, after all, we're a loving couple fresh from our second honeymoon. Surely I'd call you something besides Logan." Or jerk, or any number of other less than flattering names, she didn't add.

He leveled the full weight of that intense gaze on

her, yanking back the little bit of ground she'd gained. "Of course. I should have told you already." He flared one wide hand, indicating that she should get into the vehicle. Suddenly uncomfortable with this little war of wills, she obeyed. He closed the door firmly behind her and leaned into the open window. "Lover," he said…whispered actually. "Whenever you feel the urge to be affectionate, you can call me *Lover*."

She faced front, suddenly considerably more afraid of being alone with and this unbearably close to Logan than any threat Esteban represented. Just when she thought she'd scream in frustration, Logan drew away. She watched as he skirted the hood, thankfully without so much as a glance in her direction. Well, now, she'd asked for that one, hadn't she? It wouldn't happen again. This was going to be tough enough without playing silly little cat and mouse games. But there was just something about him that brought out the competitiveness in her, that made her want to…play.

Erin shook her head and resisted the urge to sigh. Hadn't she already learned her lesson the hard way? A girl couldn't trust a guy whose only motivation was getting the job done. And John Logan definitely fell into that category.

UP CLOSE, Medellín reminded Erin a bit of typical Western U.S. cities, except for the salsa spiciness here and there that lent the city a definite old-fashioned Latin spirit. Nestled in the hills, the landscape was lovely. The climate mild, yet balmy. Or maybe it was just the overall ambiance. Again she wondered at how this city could be home to such a brutal drug cartel. According to Logan, Esteban was the voice of authority in the cartel. Only he wasn't limiting his business to organic exports. The Department of Alcohol, Tobacco and Firearms already knew Esteban was stealing shipments of military weapons and reselling them. What they didn't know was how he was managing to slip under their security nets.

According to Logan, when none of the other Federal Agencies had been able to pinpoint the mole, his people were put on the case. And the rest, unfortunately for Erin, was history. Of course she tried to look at it from the perspective that Logan was giving her a second chance at life…the one she'd foolishly lost to the likes of her ex-fiancé. Whether she would live to enjoy her promised freedom was yet to be determined.

A few turns later and they'd moved into the seedier side of town. Medellín or Atlanta, it made no difference, all cities had their less attractive, more dangerous neighborhoods. She surveyed the run-down buildings and street people lingering beneath decrepit awnings and on street corners. Many were children, she realized with growing uneasiness. She wanted to look away, but couldn't. Their solemn faces and big eyes beckoned to her.

"Staring will only make you feel worse."

The gently spoken advice startled Erin. She turned to Logan and wondered how a man so seemingly emotionless could speak so kindly. His expression was grim.

"It's a way of life down here. Between the poverty

and the violence and the machismo in this culture, the kids are left to fend for themselves.''

She frowned. ''What do you mean by machismo?''

He glanced at her as he continued down the street. ''The fathers frequently abandon their families. They're far too cool to deal with parenting. With no welfare benefits or health care and a passel of babies, the mothers have little choice but to send their oldest kids out to help earn for the family.''

Erin's confusion deepened, as did her frown. She couldn't begin to fathom the concept. ''How could those kids back there hope to earn money? They're practically babies themselves.''

Logan stopped at a cross street. His gaze locked with hers. ''You don't want to know.''

He was right. She didn't. Her imagination conjured up enough atrocities without any help at all. Erin swallowed the sickening feeling that welled in her throat. She could have gone the rest of her life without seeing those children, but it was too late now. The haunting images would stay with her forever.

Logan eased the SUV to the curb in front of what Erin estimated to be a cantina. There was no neon sign outside broadcasting the name of the joint or the proprietor. In fact, there was no sign at all. She supposed that was a good thing since she doubted any self-respecting businessman would admit to owning the place.

''Just follow my lead.''

He said the words too quietly and without looking at her. When Logan opened his door, she opened hers.

They emerged from the vehicle slowly. Erin took her time and cautiously observed her surroundings just like Logan had taught her. *The key is in the details,* he'd repeated relentlessly during the past week's training. *Never, ever let yourself be blindsided. Stay alert. Note every single detail as if your life depended upon that one however seemingly insignificant item.*

At least a half dozen kids flocked around her before Logan reached her side of the SUV. They cried out to her. *Senorita! Senorita!* Dirty palms were outstretched. Faces were expectant...hopeful.

"Keep moving." Logan urged her toward the less than savory establishment's door.

"Can't we give them something?" she protested, looking back as he propelled her forward. "What if they're hungry?"

Logan halted abruptly and pulled her around to face him. He jerked her into an intimate embrace and whispered for her ears only, his voice savage, his words brutal. "Because we're the bad guys now. We don't care if they've eaten. Get into character, Bailey, it's show time. And I, for one, want to live to see another day."

Her breath came in sharp, rapid bursts. She wanted to tell him to forget the whole thing. That helping these children was far more important. But she knew it wouldn't matter. In the end, if they brought Esteban down, maybe it would make life better for these children. That was something, wasn't it?

Logan released her, but kept one long arm around her shoulders as he ushered her in the direction of the cantina's half-open door. Just before they stepped inside he pressed his lips to her temple and murmured, "Act like you want to be here, Baby. We've worked hard to get here."

Several heart-thumping moments passed before her eyes adjusted to the dim interior of the cantina. When they finally did, she suddenly wished they hadn't. Wooden tables and chairs, all occupied, cluttered the floor space. She decided instantly that everyone in the place looked exactly like a criminal. It wasn't so much precisely how they looked as it was the expressions on their faces. Openly challenging and just plain old mean.

A long bar sprawled across the far side of the room. Several stools were vacant and Logan headed that way. He slid onto one and pulled her between his widespread thighs in a possessive manner.

Despite the fear pumping furiously in her veins, a tiny jolt of awareness shot through her. She tensed, ready to draw away, but Logan was having no part of it. He anchored her to him with one powerful arm. She tried to relax…to lean into him, but she just couldn't do it.

He ordered a bottle of tequila. His Spanish was perfect, the accent sounded authentic. The bartender plunked the requested liquor down along with two glasses and went about his business the moment Logan deposited a crisp American bill on the counter. Ice formed in Erin's fingers, tightened like a band around her chest while no less than twenty gazes devoured her as if she were the newest entrée on the buffet.

Logan nipped her earlobe, simultaneously sending a chill over her skin and heat searing through her insides. "Smile, baby, these are our kind of people," he murmured against her skin. "We want to fit in."

She managed a smile as she reached back to stroke Logan's jaw. "Whatever you say, *Lover*," she whispered back despite the electrical surge that had almost rendered her speechless the moment her fingers made contact with his chiseled profile.

Slowly, the attention of the men gathered around the tables drifted back to their own circle of conversation. Relief made Erin weak. Logan didn't have to worry about her bolting now, she sagged against him.

"See that guy who just walked in?"

Erin leaned fully against Logan's chest so that she could look without being too obvious. Butterflies took flight in her middle at the feel of his masculine body against her back. She definitely didn't need to analyze every contour and bulge she felt pressed intimately against her. If she did...well, she wasn't going to.

"Ummm-hmmm," she purred. The guy, tall, broad-shouldered, a reject from a bad western movie, remained in the doorway for three or four seconds, then went back outside.

Logan kissed her neck. "That's our contact."

Erin turned around to face him. She braced her hands on his muscular thighs and struggled to maintain her composure in spite of how touching him that way stole her breath. "What do we do now?" She wanted to run like hell. That's what she wanted to do. Her heart pounded, as much from Logan's nearness, dammit, as from fear of what was about to take place.

Those dark eyes probed hers...read her like an open book. "We," he said with just the tiniest hint of smugness, "join him outside." His fingers splayed on her waist, then slid down her hips and molded to her bottom. He knew the effect he had on her. She could just die. How could he make her feel this way when she didn't want to? God, she was pathetic.

He kissed her lips this time, scarcely a touch, but enough to rock Erin's world all over again. The next thing she knew, he was leading her back out into the bright light of day. Her ears were ringing, her skin tingling. Fear and desire whirled inside her like hyperactive ballerinas.

She had the sudden, overwhelming urge to run or cry or both. Oh, God. She couldn't do either. She had to focus. To pay attention. Logan all but dragged her toward the waiting man at the corner where a narrow street crossed the broader one that ran in front of the cantina. Erin almost stumbled when Logan dropped a wad of crumpled bills, but he pulled her closer, forcing her to move forward with him.

Before she could tell him that he'd dropped his money, he was already in brisk conversation with the man he'd called their contact. Erin glanced back to where the money had fallen. The children who'd greeted them when they emerged from the SUV were flocked around it now.

A slow, knowing smile slid across her face. He'd dropped the money on purpose. For the children. Erin turned back to the man still clutching her hand. Maybe Logan wasn't as unfeeling as he wanted her to believe.

Maybe he was the real McCoy...a good-looking, fiercely loyal, all-American hero out to defend his country and all it stood for, determined to help her regain her freedom and see justice done.

Her smile drooped into a frown.

And maybe Santa Claus was real, too.

Chapter Five

Esteban's compound—estate, he would call it—sprawled across a ridge overlooking the valley and the one incoming road. To the rear of the property, craggy cliffs dropped a hundred meters or so. Satellite photography had already allowed Mission Recovery to determine that it would be near impossible to enter the compound from the rear. From the front or the air would be the most plausible scenario, if an insertion team survived the unavoidable confrontation since there would be absolutely no cover. The long, unpaved driveway cut through acres of strategically cleared property, negating any possibility of a surprise attack.

In Logan's opinion, men like Esteban didn't deserve to live. The simplest way to rid humankind of parasites like him was to drop a smart-bomb and clear out the whole hillside. But then they wouldn't know the one little detail that kept Esteban alive despite his numerous enemies and his horrendous trespasses against society as a whole—the man on the inside who gave him his information. That one little thing kept Logan's people from surgically removing the cancer Esteban represented.

Logan didn't want to think about the fact that this mole was almost certainly one of their own. An American in a high level position who was willing to sacrifice anything for the almighty dollar. He clenched his jaw, there would be plenty of time for garnering justice when they knew the guy's name.

Bailey was too quiet, he decided, turning his attention to the more immediate aspects of the mission. He knew she was struggling to maintain a calm facade. Trying to see things the way she would, he surveyed ground zero as they bumped up the rocky drive behind their escort. High, secure walls encircled the house and grounds. Ivy had long since overtaken the better part of the massive stone structure surrounding Esteban's private residence and command center. Ancient trees, obviously carefully protected from harm during construction, loomed tall over all else. The mansion was built of the same stone as the security wall, and topped with a red tile roof. Intelligence had estimated the house at twenty thousand square feet.

The guest house was across a wide quadrangle that served as a courtyard to the elegant house. Other smaller buildings, Logan could only guess at the use of, dotted the expansive, well-guarded property.

Case in point, the wide iron gates now opening to allow the two vehicles entrance. Once inside the compound, Bailey sat up a little straighter, peering at the opulent fountain and meticulously manicured grounds.

Large windows and arched entryways gave the house the appearance of a grand hotel.

"I never expected anything like this," Bailey said, equal measures of awe and surprise coloring her tone.

Logan braked to a stop several feet from the other vehicle and shoved the gearshift into Park. "Remember to watch what you say from this moment on," he warned quietly. "The place is most likely wired inside and out."

She nodded, eyes huge, fearful. Not for the first time since this whole thing began, Logan wished it didn't have to be this way. It was far too risky. He could take care of himself, but Bailey—he let go a long breath—she was a rookie without the proper training.

A liability to the mission…and herself.

And the only hope they had of getting this done.

She swallowed tightly. He followed the movement of delicate muscle along the slender column of her throat. "I'm ready," she said, her voice wavering just the slightest bit.

He knew he shouldn't, but he just couldn't help himself. He touched her. Reached out and stroked one soft cheek with his fingertips. "I owe you, Bailey."

She sucked in an uneven breath and he had the sudden, nearly overwhelming urge to shove the SUV back into gear and drive away as fast as he could until he got her to safety.

A sharp rap on Logan's window broke the spell he'd fallen into. "Come on, come on!" a deeply accented voice demanded. Cortez, their escort. "Didn't you two get enough of that in Bermuda? Esteban is waiting!"

Logan pushed open his door and stood. He shrugged at the impatient brute glaring at him. "With a woman like this you never get enough." He grinned at Cortez before striding around to Bailey's side of the vehicle. "Ain't that right, Baby?"

"Anything you say, Lover," she purred as she cuddled up next to him.

Cortez growled something in Spanish that Logan didn't quite catch, then led the way through the main courtyard and onto the rambling terrace. The place was even bigger than it had looked in the satellite photographs Logan had studied. Analysts had estimated the interior layout as best they could with nothing to go on but the exterior structure. It would be interesting to see how accurate their estimations were.

Bailey stuck close to him. He kept his left arm firmly around her. To make her feel more secure, he told himself. It had nothing to do with the way it simply felt right to hold her. He remembered Maverick's warning. He had to use this distracting physical attraction to his advantage. And that's all it was, basic biology...chemistry at best.

It wasn't until they actually entered the house itself that Erin felt even remotely at ease. There was something about the dozen or so armed soldiers stalking the grounds that put her on edge. Esteban's private army. She had to admit that they were the best-dressed soldiers she'd ever seen. Some sported elegant suits, and, of course, wicked looking machine guns. Others were dressed in desert camouflage, also possessing machine guns. Surprisingly, there was a pretty equal mix of

Anglos and Latinos. She hadn't really expected Esteban to put personal security in the hands of anyone other than his own people. But Logan had explained that every member of Esteban's staff—security, as well as couriers—was handpicked. Well, at least, he was an equal opportunity employer.

She forgot all about security or anything else when their escort delivered them into the parlor. She'd known from the lavish exterior that the house would be beautiful, but she would never have imagined how beautiful. The arched doorways were repeated inside the house. The wide entry hall that had brought them this far was tastefully decorated and well lit by the expansive windows, which continued throughout the house. But, here in this room, it was the splendid artwork, exquisite paintings and lovely sculptures, that established the ambiance of richness, of pure elegance.

Esteban certainly had taste, if nothing else.

"Ah, Mr. and Mrs. Wilks!"

A booming voice startled Erin from her avid interest in the décor. Fear, dark and foreboding, stole through her when she faced the man who could select art with such a discriminating eye and yet who thought nothing of killing hundreds, thousands maybe, with his illegal drugs and weapons.

He wasn't as tall as Logan, but he looked fit for a man of forty. Gray peppered his short black hair and mustache, but his equally black eyes were crystal clear and far too seeing. Even had Logan not told her anything about Esteban, Erin knew instinctively that this man was to be feared.

Logan extended his hand. "Senor Esteban, we appreciate your hospitality."

He shook Logan's hand, but quickly turned his formidable attention to Erin. "I trust the two of you enjoyed your time in Bermuda?"

Erin resisted the urge to move closer to Logan under the man's fierce analysis. He looked at her like the men in the cantina had, as if she was his for the taking. He made no attempt to hide the blatant sexual hunger in those black eyes.

"We loved every minute of it, didn't we, Baby?" Logan pulled her close against him.

Whether the move was simply to lend credibility to his act or from instinct that she needed him to do it, Erin couldn't say. She was just glad Logan had done it.

Esteban's gaze landed on Erin once more. "You changed your hair."

The statement sounded far too much like an accusation for her comfort. She searched for the right response, but came up empty.

Esteban suddenly smiled wolfishly. "I like it." He turned to Logan, his expression all business now. "We have much to discuss. Cortez will take your lovely wife to Sheila, another of my guests. Sheila will show her around and assist in settling the two of you in your quarters."

"Sounds good." Logan dropped a quick kiss on Erin's forehead. "Be good, Baby."

He released her then and, without a backward

glance, followed Esteban from the room. Leaving her completely alone with an armed stranger.

"This way, *Baby*," Cortez urged, his tone mocking.

Her heart pounding, her palms sweating, Erin ignored his remark and followed him back into the entry hall. Outside, he wound around the house to the east side. The generous terrace, its timeworn pavers lending a gracious antiquity, completely encompassed the house with wide French doors leading into the bordering rooms. She tried not to wonder where they were going...or what would happen when they got there.

Just up ahead the first woman Erin had seen in the compound sat in a thickly cushioned chair at a patio table beneath a huge tree. The tree shaded the area beyond the terrace and dappled light over the woman whose full attention, Erin noted as she neared, appeared to be focused on the long, slender cigarette in her hand. Thank God for small favors, Erin mused. She'd be much more comfortable in the presence of another woman. Especially one who didn't appear to be armed.

Cortez glanced at the seated woman with blatant disdain. "Esteban said to show her around." He promptly did an about-face and left.

Sheila shot Erin a look that was about as friendly as a pit bull. "So you're the new girl, huh?"

"That's right." Without waiting to be asked, Erin settled into one of the chairs facing her. Erin had the distinct impression an invitation would not have been forthcoming. Up close, this woman—Sheila—looked every bit as mean and cutthroat as the armed guards.

After further consideration, Erin was pretty sure Sheila wouldn't need a gun to do damage. Her long, blood-red nails and hate-filled eyes looked plenty lethal all on their own.

Sheila stubbed out her cigarette and glared at Erin. "Just remember that I was here first. Rank has its privileges. Don't you go thinking that just because you're new that you can move in on my territory."

Erin frowned, hoping to look innocent rather than confused. "I'm not sure I'm following you."

That only seemed to infuriate Sheila all the more. "I'm Esteban's favorite." She smiled, an exceedingly unpleasant gesture. "Other than his own sister, I've been the only woman living here for over a year. Don't go thinking your presence is going to change anything." She waved her hand in dismissal. "You won't last a week," she predicted.

The distant hum of fear in Erin's ears didn't help. Thankfully she managed to maintain a fairly calm exterior. "Great ring," she said, instead of arguing with the woman. Changing the subject seemed prudent and Erin couldn't help noticing the large rock on Sheila's left ring finger when she started waving her arms around. The narrow accompanying gold band was rather plain next to the huge diamond.

"You're married?" Erin went on. Whoever was saddled with this Class A bitch surely lived a life of misery. Then again, considering the sort hanging out around this place, the two probably deserved each other.

"Of course." Sheila adopted a smug face. "His

name is Larry. You'll meet him eventually.'' She patted her thick auburn tresses. ''He has a thing for redheads.'' She glowered at Erin. ''Your color job sucks. I hope you didn't pay the moron who did it.''

It wasn't until that moment that Erin realized how well she'd fooled them all. They'd all seen Jess's picture or maybe they'd even seen her in real life, sans the introductions, of course. And not one of them suspected that Erin wasn't Jess. That blond was her natural hair color. Logan's plan had worked!

The epiphany shook her just a little.

Erin shrugged. ''I decided I wanted to see if blondes really did have more fun.''

Sheila rolled her eyes. ''You *really* are stupid, aren't you? Do you really think blond hair is the only criteria for seducing a man like Esteban?''

Before Erin could think of an appropriate comeback, Sheila pushed to her feet, an amazing accomplishment in Erin's opinion considering the woman's short skirt was tight enough to cut off the circulation to her legs.

''Come on,'' Sheila ordered. ''I'll give you the grand tour. Though I doubt you'll last long enough to need it.''

Erin followed her, wondering if she really looked that innocent and how Sheila walked in those shoes. Her red hair bounced around her shoulders and every so often she tossed her head so it flew around like a wild horse's mane. Erin decided that Sheila did that little number whenever they passed a group of guards just to get their attention. Not that it was really necessary. The woman was fashionably tall and had one of those model thin figures. Erin, on the other hand, was kind of short and not exactly fat, but she did have some meat on her bones.

She absolutely hated these too-snug jeans and the cropped top. But she had to stay in character. That was her job. It would keep her alive and help regain her freedom.

"This is the guest house," Sheila explained disinterestedly as they approached a small two-story building. It looked older than the house. The ivy-covered stone lessened its ominous appearance. "You'll bunk here," Sheila added as she opened the door.

Inside, a wide stairwell led up to the second floor. Two doors flanked each side of the stairwell, downstairs and up.

"This one's yours." Sheila gestured to the first door on the right, then walked over and opened it. "Your bags are already here."

Erin followed her inside and, sure enough, the two duffels were lying in the middle of the floor. She knew instantly that they had been searched. The careless lumps and bulges left by the search were hard to miss.

"Most of the security guys live in the barracks." Sheila walked over to the front window and pointed across the backyard. "There's ten. You'll meet them all at one time or another around the dinner table." She turned back to Erin, arms folded over her store-bought bosom. "Esteban insists we eat together as often as possible. You'll find he has a few other quirks, but I'll let you discover those for yourself."

Sheila started toward the door. "Let me know if you need anything else," she tossed over her shoulder. "I'm upstairs and across the hall, front apartment." At the door she turned back to Erin and studied her for one endless beat. "I don't like you, *Baby*," she all but ground out. "Stay out of my way and we'll get along just fine."

She slammed the door behind her.

Erin exhaled a shaky breath. She'd been here barely half an hour and she'd made an enemy already. And, wow, what a grand tour.

She peered out the window and for the first time allowed all that she saw to sink in. A couple of guards paced the eastern perimeter of the house, their lethal machine guns swinging from shoulder straps. A turret of sorts jutted above the rooftop on the west side of the house. It didn't take a military strategist to figure out that it was a security station. From that level one would be able to see for miles out over the valley below. Esteban would know of any unexpected presence ten or fifteen minutes before anyone arrived at his gate.

More guards were stationed at the massive gate. Everyone inside these walls was, in effect, a prisoner. The walls immediately began to close in around her. She hugged herself and squeezed her eyes shut, fought the fear and the vertigo that always accompanied one of her bouts with claustrophobia. She battled the urge to run out the door. No wrong moves, Logan had said. Appearances were everything.

Erin took long, deep breaths until she got the wave

of panic under control. When the shakes had subsided she opened her eyes once more. All she had to do was keep it together. Logan would take care of the rest. She didn't actually have to do anything at this point…just keep up the appearance of the loving wife. A new kind of shiver rushed through her at that last thought, but she stiffened her spine against it.

She had work to do. Putting the reality of her circumstances out of her mind, she decided to familiarize herself with their temporary living quarters. She could unpack and then maybe take a walk around the grounds if it was permitted. She hadn't thought to ask Sheila about that. Maybe she'd just ask one of the guards. Avoiding Sheila felt like the wise thing to do.

In the main room, there was a large, overstuffed sofa and matching chair, a couple of tables and one painting. A television and DVD player occupied one corner of the room, while a bookcase with, unbelievably, a number of hardback books on its shelves filled the other. Between the two was an adobe fireplace that made the room cozy and even welcoming. Erin almost muttered something negative, but caught herself. Logan had warned her that their room would likely be bugged. She suddenly wondered if there would be cameras, too. She shuddered at the possibility. This little adventure might turn out to be worse than prison.

An efficiency kitchen and small dining room lay beyond the front room. There was nothing spectacular about either, simple and neat. She opened a few cabinet doors and then the fridge. Well stocked, she noted with surprise.

She located the bathroom and bedroom next. The bathroom was a bit more luxurious than the kitchen. There was a large whirlpool tub and a huge walk-in shower. The bedroom, though certainly comfortable enough, had only one large bed. She sighed and dropped onto the foot of it. She and Logan were supposed to be man and wife. She glanced at the narrow gold band on her left ring finger. Except she wasn't sure she could deal with sleeping in the same bed with him. Then again, it wasn't like she could refuse. It would look strange, and they couldn't risk that.

No point fretting over the unavoidable, she reasoned. She might as well get past it. With that firmly resolved in her mind, Erin dragged the duffels into the bedroom, her own first and then Logan's.

She surveyed the mirrored dresser and matching bureau and decided she'd take the dresser. Staying busy would keep her thoughts off this place and Esteban. While she worked, she plotted Jeff's fall. Erin smiled. Now there was a distraction.

By the time she had neatly stored her things, she'd devised a master plan for taking Jeff down. She'd provoke him into confessing while Logan taped the whole thing. She frowned and glanced at the digital clock on the bedside table. Speaking of Logan, where was he?

She supposed that he and Esteban had important business to discuss, but surely it didn't take this long. With a shrug she opened Logan's duffel. She was his wife after all, right? Putting his things away would fall under that job description.

A person could tell a lot by the way a man dressed.

With Jeff, he'd been all flash and charm. Always perfectly dressed, if not in a suit, then in designer khakis and a sweater. Never, ever would he have been caught dead—the mere idea made her a little giddy—in T-shirts and mere jeans.

But Logan, he wasn't like that at all. His jeans were well-worn. She smoothed her hand over the pair she'd just taken from the duffel. He didn't need fancy labels to give him confidence, she decided as she arranged his jeans in one of the bureau drawers. He was confident enough in himself that he didn't have to belittle others to feel good about who he was. She cringed now when she thought of all the times she'd let her former fiancé make her feel unworthy, both professionally and personally.

That would never happen again. She pushed the drawer closed and moved on to the shirts. After this, no one would ever be able to tell her that she couldn't do anything she set her mind to. No way.

By the time Logan's button-down shirts were all hanging in the closet, she'd been dancing and singing around the room. She hoped Esteban or whoever was listening enjoyed her tone-deaf renditions.

She reached into the duffel, all the way to the bottom, and came up empty-handed. A frown furrowed its way across her brow. Jeans, shirts, T-shirts, socks…what about underwear?

Erin turned the bag upside down and shook it. She checked for hidden zippers. Nothing. She stored the empty duffels in the closet and leaned against the closed door for a second to consider where she hadn't looked. They'd brought no other bags with them that she recalled. Nope, she was sure of it. The two duffels were it.

One eyebrow winged above the other. Maybe he didn't wear shorts or briefs...or boxers. Her mouth went a little dry and she swallowed convulsively. That was ridiculous, everyone wore underwear. She glanced around the room, on the bed, across the carpeted floor. Apparently Logan didn't...unless he simply forgot to pack them. Nah, he was too detailed to forget something like that. He'd even remembered to bring along dental floss. A man who packed his dental floss definitely packed his shorts...if he wore them.

The image of Logan in the buff immediately filled her head.

Erin's eyes widened. Time for that walk now. She made a quick stop in the bathroom and then checked out her new hairdo. It was a little too punkish for her taste, but she supposed it went with the outfit.

Whatever.

It was only acting. Actors and actresses had to dress the part, as well as play it.

The sun was straight up noon when she stepped outside once more. It glinted off the red tiled roof and the shimmering water in the large fountain halfway between the house and the guest house she'd just exited. The leaves of the trees shifted in the gentle breeze. The climate here was perfect. A little cool early in the mornings, she recalled, but absolutely gorgeous now—as was this place. It amazed her all over again that such evil could exist within the walls of this magnificent estate.

Erin studied the high, ivy covered walls and the tastefully placed shrubbery. Stone walks and blooming flowers of a variety she'd never seen before spilled out before her, inviting one and all. At the rear of the house, she saw that a guard tower had been built into the security wall. Just like in medieval days, she mused. Another bubbling fountain and more seating for entertaining or simply conducting meetings. At the rear of the house, the first floor looked as if it was constructed completely of glass. One look beyond the wall and she realized why that was. The ragged line of the Andes lay in the distance. Their cloud-covered peaks more grand than any painting. The view was awesome.

Oh, yes, Esteban had taste, but lacked heart or even basic human compassion. He was evil. If Logan's mission was successful, that evil would be eliminated.

A frown tugged at her again. Where was Logan? She scanned the courtyard all the way to the towering walls of the fence. No one, except the ever present guards. A sinking feeling dragged the bottom out of Erin's stomach. Where was everyone? Had something happened and she'd missed it? She hadn't heard any gunfire or shouting or anything at all. Of course she had been preoccupied with singing.

What if something had happened to Logan?

Fear snaked its way around her throat.

What if their cover had been blown already?

A rapid succession of automatic gunfire erupted in

the distance. Erin jumped behind the nearest tree. Her heart lunged into her throat. She could scarcely breathe. Where was Logan? Where had those shots come from?

"You must return to your quarters."

Erin spun toward the unfamiliar male voice.

"Where's Logan?" she demanded, her voice thin.

"Go back to your quarters," the man ordered, his accented tone lethal. *"Now."*

No fear. She had to stay in character. Jess would show no fear. Erin had to prove to Logan that she could do this. No, no, no! She had to prove to *herself* that she could do it

Erin squared her shoulders and lifted her chin. "I'm not going anywhere until you tell me what's going on."

He was too fast for her. She felt the blow, but her brain couldn't quite assimilate what she saw. One second he was glaring down at her, the next the butt of his weapon was coming at her.

The world went unexpectedly black.

Chapter Six

"These three men should be examples to all of you," Esteban roared, fury, hatred blazing in his eyes.

He paced before Logan and the others, his recent kills having done nothing to abate his anger. Logan was well aware of his famous tantrums. The display he'd just witnessed only made him despise Esteban all the more. He'd cut down three members of his personal army as they pled for their lives. Logan had no way of knowing what evidence Esteban had against them. Whatever it was, it appeared to be enough to ignite one of his rampages.

Logan usually didn't waste sympathy on scumbags. Everyone here had signed on with a full understanding of how things worked and the risk involved. Pissing off the boss by getting greedy or running one's mouth was outright asking for trouble. Disloyalty was not tolerated in Esteban's circle. Logan knew it, those standing on either side of him knew it and so had the dead men.

Still, he hated to see human life thrown away like yesterday's trash. It made him sick to his stomach to be a part of this even for a few days. His gaze landed on the man still pacing like an agitated beast. But if pretending to be a part of this group would bring down this bastard, Logan could tolerate most anything.

"Disloyalty is punishable by death." Esteban paused in front of one of his most loyal followers. "Is that not true, my old friend?"

"That's a fact, *jefe*."

Larry Watters. Former military. Wanted in Texas for first degree murder. He and his wife had been on Esteban's payroll for over a year now. Just the guy Logan needed to get close to.

"And you, my newest friend—" Esteban stopped next in front of Logan "—do you have any questions?"

Logan hitched up one corner of his mouth in a good old boy smile and looked directly into the eyes of his new boss, his *jefe*. "Just one. When do we eat?"

Esteban's gaze held his for an endless moment, his intense expression unreadable. Absolute silence fell around them. Logan held his ground, his own gaze unwavering, never leaving the other man's.

Esteban burst into laughter. The others followed suit, like puppets on a string. Logan chuckled. He'd taken a chance, and he'd not only survived, he'd turned the tide of one of Esteban's rampages. He wondered how many here had been successful at that…had even attempted it? Logan's heart rate returned to normal as he relaxed. Now, if only he'd accomplished the first of his goals…

"You are right, my new friend, Logan." Esteban

clapped him on the back and ushered him away from the scene of the crime. "It is well past noon. I would like to have you and your lovely wife join me for lunch."

Oh, yes. He was in. Logan nodded. "My wife will be thrilled." He leaned a bit closer to Esteban. "She's an art buff to the max." Logan grinned. "But not to worry, she stopped *collecting* after we met."

Esteban laughed again. "Collecting, eh? I must show her my private collection. I am sure she will love it."

A predatory gleam sprang to life in the older man's eyes. Logan bared his teeth to keep up the illusion of a smile. "How kind of you." He would have to warn Bailey to watch her step with Esteban. Logan had just unwittingly made her a prime target of his other widely acclaimed bad habit—womanizing.

When Logan reached their assigned quarters he was surprised to find it bone-chillingly quiet. He went on instant alert. Where the hell was Bailey? Fear nagged at him, but he pushed it away.

Silently, he moved through the front room. The place appeared untouched. There were no signs of struggle. There was no sound—then he heard something. He paused near the bedroom door and listened. A softly muttered curse echoed from beyond the room. He headed toward the closed bathroom door. He reached for the knob, but hesitated. Thinking better of simply bursting in, he rapped on the polished wood surface. The last thing he wanted to do was startle her. She might say or do something out of character.

"Baby, you in there?"

There was a lengthy pause, then she called out through the door, "I'll be out in a minute."

Logan tensed. Something was wrong. He reached for the knob again. Was she falling apart already? "I'm coming in."

He pushed the door open and came face-to-face with a trembling Bailey. She held a makeshift ice pack against her left temple. A bruise was darkening beneath her eye and her face looked red from crying.

"It's nothing," she said quickly, her voice as shaky as the rest of her. She retreated a step.

Fury exploded inside Logan. "What the hell happened?" His first thought was that he would kill the person responsible for this.

She held up a hand to keep him at bay, but he ignored it, moving closer. "I'm fine, really." She blinked rapidly at the new surge of tears he saw welling in those luminous violet eyes.

When he'd backed her against the far wall and she could run no further, he glared down at her, too angry to comfort her at the moment. "Tell me what happened."

She moistened those full lips and tried to take a breath, which only caught in her chest, the way it would when someone had cried for too long. "I decided to take a walk around the grounds." She brushed at the tears with the back of her free hand. "I heard the gunshots and I was worried..." She blinked some more and cleared her throat. "One of the guards told me to come back here, but I wanted to make sure you…you were all right.'' She shrugged halfheartedly. "Apparently he took my response to his order as insubordination.''

Logan's fury morphed into unadulterated rage. "He hit you?''

She nodded.

A single tear rolled down her cheek.

Logan snapped.

"I'll talk to Esteban about this,'' he said tightly. He pulled her hand away and grimaced at the size on the lump on the side of her head. The bruise ran from the hairline at her temple to the corner of her left eye. "And then I'm going to kill the guy who did this.''

He knew he was beyond rational thinking. He also knew he was overreacting. But he couldn't slow the emotions raging out of control inside him. He gently caressed her injured cheek. "Son of a bitch,'' he muttered.

"No. Forget about it. I should have listened to him. It was my mistake.'' She clutched his hand tightly, desperately in hers and pulled it away from the evidence of the brutality she'd endured. "Don't make it worse…I don't…'' Her voice trailed off. She squeezed her eyes shut. "I don't want to make trouble.''

He had to do something. He pulled her into his arms and held her tightly to him. She felt soft and oh so fragile in his hold. There wasn't anything he could risk saying for fear of being overheard. And even if he dared, how could he make this right? He'd known this would be the way of it. No one in this place could be trusted. The only thing he could hope for was to keep her safe from anything worse. She had no way of understanding this world…and he couldn't fully protect her from these sleazebags. They were surrounded by people who killed for the sport of it more often than out of necessity. Brutality was their way of life. Any one of Esteban's chosen ones would kill for him… would die for him without blinking an eye.

There was no way to shield an innocent like the woman he held in his arms from the ugliness of Esteban's world. Logan closed his eyes and made a silent promise to her. He would find a way to keep her safe.

One way or another.

ERIN HAD NEVER been so relieved in her entire life to see anyone as she was to see Logan. She'd feared the worst. Worried that he was dead and she would be next. When she'd regained consciousness the guard had already slung her over his shoulder and had almost gotten her back to their quarters. She'd kicked and pounded with her fists until he'd put her down. She'd had a hell of a time getting rid of him at the door. Threatening to scream had done the trick. She shuddered when she considered what he would likely have done to her had he gotten her inside where no one would hear her scream before she came to.

Logan had been right. She hadn't had a clue just how brutal these people were. She'd instinctively known better than to tell him what trouble she'd had getting rid of the guard. Logan's possessiveness surprised her. Or maybe he just felt responsible for her general safety. That was the most likely case, she decided. Still, his reaction had been fiercer than she'd expected.

Logan had explained in as little detail as possible that the gunfire had been Esteban executing three traitors. She shuddered again. God, how long would they live before someone discovered the truth about them? It wasn't until she'd heard those gunshots that she realized just how much danger she and Logan really were in. This was far worse than anything she had imagined. Even though Logan had tried to warn her, she couldn't have possibly anticipated this reality.

LATER, AS THEY entered the main house, Erin prayed that this unexpected invitation wasn't further cause for concern. Logan insisted it was a good sign, if she'd read between the lines accurately. They had to be extremely careful what they said and whispering would appear suspicious. The only thing Erin could do was hope for the best. They were here now. Whatever happened, would happen.

She did feel safe as long as Logan was nearby. She glanced at the silent man at her side. Did all of his missions require that he enter this kind of lethal environment? Long-term survival in his line of work seemed slim at best. Her respect for him had grown immensely over the past few hours. Logan had to be very good at his work...otherwise they'd both be dead already.

If she were back in Atlanta in that cell, she might be dead by now as well, considering the guard and the inmate who'd had it in for her. She wondered again how Logan had known about her troubles in prison. Maybe he'd asked other inmates about her. One of them might have overheard something. Erin glanced around the elaborately furnished hall as they continued through the house toward the dining room. At least here she had a chance.

When she noticed the two armed guards waiting on either side of the dining room entrance, Erin amended that last statement. One thing was certain, they definitely weren't in Kansas anymore and she felt exactly like Dorothy in *The Wizard of Oz*.

"Ah, here they are!" Esteban stood from his position at the head of the table. "Please have a seat." He waved his hand with a flourish to indicate the expansive and elegantly laden dining table. "You've already met the Watterses."

Sheila and her husband were seated on the far side of the table. Sheila gave Erin a what-the-hell-happened-to-you look. Her husband appeared indifferent. Cortez stood near Esteban, his weapon held firmly in front of him. Another woman, thirty-five maybe, the well-dressed, sophisticated type, sat at the opposite end of the table from Esteban. Erin immediately noted the resemblance.

"And may I present to you, my beloved sister, Maria," Esteban announced proudly. He literally beamed with awe or respect...something on that order.

Logan made some acknowledging comment as the woman nodded to him and then to Erin. Their eyes met and Erin had the oddest feeling. As if the woman saw right into her soul. She shook off the eerie sensation. She was a little too punchy after the incident with the butt of a rifle.

Logan held her chair as Erin settled into it, then he sat down beside her. She forced herself to eat as the meal began, despite the fist of fear pressing firmly into her stomach. The discussion at the table remained light. Politics, weather, even the latest movie premieres were among the topics. Just like the Brady bunch, Erin mused dryly.

Finally, after the last course, Esteban rose from his chair. "Come to me, Sara."

It took a couple of tension-filled seconds for Erin to realize he was speaking to her. He gestured for her to come when her gaze belatedly collided with his. No fear, she reminded herself, though it was hard to hear even her own thoughts when the blood roared in her ears like a freight train. Logan immediately stood and turned to Esteban.

"I won't tolerate—"

"It's all right, my friend," he said to Logan, cutting off his angry words, then looked back to Erin. "Come."

Logan pulled out her chair and she rose on shaky legs. His gaze locked with hers for one heart-stopping second. He tried to reassure her with his eyes, but even the promise in that dark, dark gaze couldn't alleviate the anxiety mushrooming inside her. As she moved around him, Logan resumed his seat, but she knew he didn't take his eyes off her because she could feel him watching her.

She held herself straight in spite of the fear pumping

through her veins. "Yes?" she said when she paused next to the man who had the power to end her life here and now.

Esteban placed a hand at the small of her back. She gritted her teeth against the shiver that threatened. Esteban gestured to the far side of the room. "Is this the man who hit you today?"

Shock radiated through Erin as the guard who'd dazed her entered the room. He didn't look so fierce now, unarmed and with another guard propelling him forward. He looked as scared as hell—sort of like she felt at the moment. The man stopped on the opposite side of Esteban. He looked sickly pale for a man of Latin heritage.

"His name is Manuel. Is he the one?" Esteban asked again, the slightest hint of impatience in his tone.

Erin looked from Esteban to Manuel and then back. "Yes."

Esteban turned to Cortez who remained on sentry detail right behind his lord and master. Esteban extended his hand. *"La arma, por favor?"*

Cortez placed a gleaming silver handgun in Esteban's outstretched palm. Esteban shifted his attention back to Erin. "This man hurt you, did he not?"

Uncertainty pulsed in time with the racing of her heart. She moistened her lips and did the only thing she could, she told the truth. "Yes."

Esteban offered her the weapon. "Then he deserves to die. Kill him."

Terror exploded in her chest. She couldn't breathe.

Esteban's black gaze bore down on her. She knew Logan was behind her, watching, most likely poised to intervene. But that would blow their cover. The memory of pulling that trigger with the weapon aimed at Logan rocketed to the forefront of her mind. But that had been a completely different situation. She'd been angry...now she was just plain scared.

She didn't have to look to know that everyone, including Logan, was waiting...watching.

"No."

The solitary word had come from her.

Esteban's intense expression shifted to incredulity.

Before he could demand that she obey him, Erin rushed to explain, "I made a mistake." She glanced at the man expecting to die any moment. "He asked me to return to my quarters and I refused." She swallowed, difficult as that proved. "It was my fault. He was only doing his job."

No one moved. No one spoke for what felt like an eternity. Her heart all but stopped beating.

Esteban passed the weapon back to Cortez. He didn't quite smile, but got close. "You are a very brave woman, my dear." He glanced disdainfully at the waiting guard. "And you saved Manuel's life. *Vaya!*" The guard obeyed the command to go, rushing away, nearly stumbling in his haste.

Erin felt weak with relief. A couple more seconds of that kind of stress and she'd surely have had a heart attack.

Esteban glanced at those still seated. "Have a pleasant afternoon," he said in dismissal. He turned his

attention back to Erin when she would have backed
away. "Your husband tells me you have a weakness
for fine art."

"It's my one weakness," Erin admitted. Back in her
college days she'd spent most of her free time in one
museum or the other. It cleared her head, helped her
think better. But she hadn't realized Logan knew that.
A tiny frown marred her brow. Or maybe she'd told
him and forgotten. His questioning had been relentless
the first couple days of training. Then again, he
seemed to know everything whether she told him or
not.

Esteban gave her the full body once over with that
devilish gaze. "Just one weakness?"

Before Erin could respond, Esteban continued,
"Larry, entertain our new friend Logan while the
lovely lady and I visit the gallery."

Logan's gaze didn't leave hers until Esteban had
ushered her from the room. Logan looked less than
happy about the situation, but what was she supposed
to do?

"The east wing is my personal suite," Esteban was
saying as they ascended the wide, curving staircase.

Erin snapped to attention. Though she was scared
to death, she knew she had to remain calm on the
outside at least…had to pay attention. Details, she reminded herself. It was the little things that made the
difference.

"Your home is amazing," she heard herself say.
Good, she thought. Pump up his ego. A man like him
thrived on control and status.

He paused on the second story landing and peered down at her with an undeniable hunger in his eyes. "I am fortunate to have many beautiful things in my life."

When the moment dragged on too long, she interjected, "How long have you been collecting?"

He started forward once more. Erin remembered to breathe. "Only for a few years, but my collection is extensive."

"I can't wait to see it," she enthused. Admiring good art would likely be the one highlight in this whole stinking mission.

"You intrigue me greatly, my dear," he said as he hesitated near an intricately carved set of double doors. "A thief, a courier of various, shall we say, forbidden merchandise…and yet you would risk my wrath to save the life of a mere expendable guard."

Uh-oh. Was that a compliment or a masterfully disguised accusation? Erin tensed inwardly. "I'm many things, Senor Esteban, but a liar I'm not. I tell it the way I see it."

He smiled. "Indeed."

A FULL HOUR had passed. Logan and Larry had parted ways fifteen minutes ago. Logan had spent every second worrying about Bailey and, since returning to their quarters, walking the damned floors.

Dammit, they were barely in the door and already things were going to hell. He could only hope that Bailey was holding her own with Esteban. Fury slashed through Logan all over again. He didn't want Esteban or anyone else touching her.

Logan swore hotly. Jealousy, possessiveness—neither of those things was supposed to play into this. They had a job to do. His only concerns were accomplishing the mission and keeping Bailey alive—in that order.

But he couldn't help himself. He couldn't stop thinking about the way Esteban had looked at her...the way he'd touched her. Logan swore again. He had to regain his perspective here. There were far too many other concerns to focus too much energy on Esteban's infatuation with Bailey.

Yeah, right.

Then why the hell was he ready to tear the man apart with his bare hands? Logan stopped in the middle of the room and plowed his fingers through his hair. He ordered himself to be calm. This was not an appropriate reaction to the day's events. He'd lost his perspective entirely.

The sound of the door opening jerked his attention in that direction. Bailey walked in and closed the door behind her.

Logan gritted his teeth until he'd formed an appropriate response. "Where the hell have you been for an entire hour?"

Bailey looked startled. Good. He wanted her afraid. If she got too cocky, she'd screw up. Then he realized his mistake and tapped his ear in reminder.

"You know where I've been," she said carefully,

obviously understanding his reminding gesture that their every word was likely being monitored.

"Did you sleep with him?" he demanded, moving toward her, the fury he could not contain hardening the features of his face, tensing his muscles.

She frowned, confused or surprised, or maybe both. "What?"

He stopped right in front of her and glared down at her, his emotions far too real for comfort. "I asked, did you sleep with him?"

"Of course not. Are you insane? We just looked at his artwork. He has a great collection. Even has a Monet."

"If you let him touch you…" Logan warned, his gaze relaying the rest of what he wanted to say.

"Get real," Erin said, her tone turning seductive. For those listening, Logan guessed. "You're the only man for me." She moved against him. "Don't you know that by now, lover?"

Logan's tense muscles grew even more rigid. It wasn't real, he reminded himself. He knew it wasn't. But it damn sure felt real to his lower anatomy. "All right," he relented. "Just remember that."

She looped her arms around his neck and made a *tsking* sound. "Now how could I forget?"

Logan wanted to kiss her again. He wanted it desperately. His arms went around her waist and he pulled her hard against his hips. Her eyes widened with the realization that he was as hard as a rock and there was no hiding it.

An abrupt pounding on the door shattered the spell.

Logan drew back, thankful for the interruption that had prevented him from making a complete fool of himself. He set Bailey aside and jerked the door open.

"What?" he demanded.

It was Cortez.

"Esteban wants to see you in the strategy room. Now." He glanced past Logan. "Bring her, too."

THE STRATEGY ROOM looked like a typical conference room to Erin. There was a long polished table surrounded by chairs, a teleconferencing unit in the center of the table, and a large projection screen on the far wall. Near the big screen was a huge map of North and South America. Pushpins of various colors were placed in strategic locations. Near the double doors that opened into the room was a sideboard complete with silver tray and crystal decanters of liquor. A humidor sat nearby, no doubt filled with the finest cigars available.

Cortez accompanied Esteban, as usual. Larry and Sheila were present, as well as two men Erin had not yet met. Erin wondered who else around here she hadn't met. Logan had briefed her on Esteban's top echelon, but she hadn't had the chance to put faces with names. She wanted to know more about the sister who'd sat silently through the events at the one meal they had shared. She hadn't spoken one word. And Logan had barely mentioned her prior to their arrival in Colombia. There was something about her…something more than her resemblance to her big brother.

Esteban pointed to Texas on the map. "There is a

new shipment of military arms arriving tomorrow. We will intercept it here." He tapped a spot west of San Antonio. "We have a twenty-minute window. There is no room for error. Hector and Carlos will take lead."

Hector and Carlos? Oh, yeah. Erin remembered the names. They were the Caldarone brothers. Hector was the oldest, but Carlos was the one with the brains. Just two more on the top of the food chain around here. A den of venomous snakes, Erin decided. These guys didn't give any advance warning either before they struck. She touched her tender lump. She knew that first hand.

"Logan," Esteban continued, "you and Sara will provide backup."

A new kind of tension coiled inside Erin.

"No problem," Logan said offhandedly.

Esteban fixed him with a meaningful look. "We'll see just how good the two of you really are." He flicked a glance in Erin's direction. "I certainly hope you can live up to the reputation which preceded you." Despite the thinly veiled threat, the man smiled.

Logan propped his arms on the table and leaned forward. "You won't be disappointed."

Erin studied her make-believe husband's profile. So confident...so true to his cover. They'd barely been here a day and already she was struggling to keep pace with the reputation Logan and his partner had worked for months to establish, earning themselves this personal invitation into Esteban's world. How on earth would she ever pull off that kind of act when the chips were down come tomorrow morning? She would need all the good luck fate could afford to lend her.

Everything inside her stilled. Then again, tomorrow morning might just turn out to be the rest of her life anyway. But tonight…well that was a different story. Tonight was approaching rapidly and she had to spend it with Logan.

In the same quarters.

In the same bed.

She was going to need a lot more than luck to get her through this night.

Chapter Seven

As the night grayed into dawn, Logan lay awake for a long while before taking a deep breath. Bailey was snuggled against him like a sleeping kitten. His arms had somehow gotten wound around her during the night. There was no way he could move or breathe deeply that wouldn't rouse her—*arouse* him—further.

A feather soft beam of light sifted through the wooden shutters and fell across her face. Logan had forced his eyes to remain closed for a time, in a futile attempt to keep the thoughts he shouldn't be having at bay. No such luck. He peered down at the sleeping woman with a fascination that was way beyond his control.

It was easy now to pinpoint the differences between her and Jess. Erin Bailey was much softer and definitely sweeter. Her mouth was wider, fuller. His loins tightened as he considered that lush mouth. No matter that her ex-fiancé had taken extreme advantage of her, she harbored none of the real cynicism second nature in Logan's line of work. She was a true innocent. She still believed that most people were good and meant well. Though she would adamantly deny the charge, she trusted far too readily on most levels.

She shifted in his arms, burrowing more fully against him. He almost groaned with the ache of wanting her. She was soft, and ripe with feminine curves. The feel of her, hell, just looking at her drove him crazy.

Another undeniable difference.

Jess had never turned him on this way. Had never made him want her physically...sexually. Even fully dressed, this woman got to him. She'd foregone the one flimsy nightgown that had been provided with her wardrobe and opted to put her clothes back on after staying in the bathroom for more than an hour pretending to take a leisurely soak. She'd been delaying the inevitable.

Sleeping with him.

He'd put her comfort before his own and slept in his jeans. The thin layer of worn fabric had done little to discourage his body's response to hers.

His arm rested against Bailey's small, pert breasts. The urge to move more firmly against them, to lower his hand there was nearly overwhelming. It wouldn't be right. She was asleep. He'd be taking advantage. His gaze traveled up the length of her slender throat, then the curve of her cheek where long lashes lay against pale, delicate skin. He frowned at the red and purple bruise beneath the corner of her left eye. Outrage boiled up inside him and it took every ounce of control he possessed not to get up and go beat the hell out of the man responsible for it.

His frown relaxed when he considered how effectively she had handled herself when Esteban ordered her to kill Manuel. Whether it was dumb luck or brilliant strategy, she'd outmaneuvered the man.

Esteban had been amused...and pleased. A crease of concern edged across Logan's brow as he considered that last part. He'd noticed more than once the way Esteban looked at Erin—Bailey, he amended. The professional in him wanted to pursue that avenue, to see how close she could get to the man. But another part of him, a much less rational part wanted her to give Esteban a wide berth. Logan would like nothing better than for her to stay away from the bastard. But that would defeat the purpose of the mission.

And the mission had to be priority one.

She stirred, her eyes slowly opening. He watched the confusion, then the realization flash in those violet depths. He felt her body tense. Her gaze lifted to meet his and the hunger he saw there weakened his resolve to keep this thing between them strictly professional.

"Good morning," she murmured, her voice still thick with sleep or maybe something else he didn't want to name.

"Morning."

"Is it time to go yet?"

He saw the desire in her eyes take a back seat to fear as yesterday's events reeled through her mind. They had a run today. It would be dangerous and it would be her first. Then again, if she feigned an illness...

She wriggled from his hold and scooted to the edge

of the bed. "We'd better get a move on," she said deliberately as if she'd read his mind.

He sat up, still studying her. She looked so damned sexy all rumpled and with her hair tousled. But he wasn't supposed to look at her that way except to lend credibility to their cover. And he wasn't the only one looking. He was shirtless and her gaze had flown instantly to his bare chest when he rose up from the mound of pillows. She leaped to her feet as if realizing she'd been caught in the act.

"I'll make coffee while you..." She backed toward the door, looking anywhere but at him. "You can take a shower or whatever." She gestured vaguely, pivoted on her heel and rushed out of the room.

He threw back the coverlet and pushed up from the warm bed. This was a hell of a way to start the day. Him aching with need and her running like a scared rabbit.

Logan suddenly wondered who scared Erin Bailey the most, him or Esteban? Better he didn't know, he supposed as he diverted his thoughts to the Caldarone brothers and the business at hand.

Erin shoved the carafe beneath the brew basket and punched the on button. She silently cursed herself for being such an idiot. This was ridiculous. She wasn't supposed to be falling for the guy like this. Just a few days ago she'd hated him for pushing her so hard, for making her do things she didn't want to do. And here she was going ga-ga over his bare chest.

Heaving a disgusted sigh she crossed her arms over her chest and leaned against the sink. Well, it actually started last night, she admitted. She'd stayed in the bathroom after her bath until the idea of remaining behind the closed door a moment longer had gone beyond rational behavior. She'd known the time would come when she'd have to sleep in the same bed with Logan, and still she hadn't been prepared.

Although he was already in bed and covered to the waist, she glimpsed that impressive chest from the corner of her eye. She looked away immediately, climbed beneath the covers fully dressed and turned out the light.

She felt sure he thought she was nuts or just plain silly for not using the nightgown provided. But it was entirely too slinky, too revealing. She just couldn't do it. Not with her already wrestling with feelings that should never have entered into this relationship. This was business...a working relationship, nothing more. They had an arrangement. She would act out her little part, Logan would nail the bad guy and then they'd shake hands and go their separate ways.

This—she inventoried the varied and fierce effect he had on her, including a rapid hammering in her chest, a hot throbbing between her thighs, and butterflies in her stomach—was not supposed to happen. Hadn't she learned anything about men? Obviously not.

She'd awakened in his arms and wanting a lot more than just to be held by him.

She was hopeless!

And then there was Esteban. He'd flagrantly flirted with her. Hadn't missed an opportunity to turn an innocent remark into an innuendo or a touch into a caress. The man was shameless. Then, what could one expect from a drug-smuggling, gun-running killer?

God Almighty, what was she doing here?

Oh, yes, freedom…the pursuit of happiness.

Considering the first twenty-four hours of her assignment, she doubted she'd live to enjoy either.

When she was certain Logan was in the shower and there wouldn't be any chance of him coming back into the room, Erin hurriedly dressed in a fresh outfit. Jeans that were worn and faded and rode low on her hips. A tight ribbed sleeveless top that didn't make it all the way to the waist of her jeans and the expensive running shoes that were the only part of her wardrobe that she had been allowed to select.

She brushed her hair and fingered gel into the top layers the way Ramon had shown her to give it lift. The spikes were out as far as she was concerned. This would have to do. Women changed their hairstyles, as well as the color, when the mood struck them. Besides, she had a lot more to worry about today than how her hair looked. She glanced at the weapons lying on the dresser. The black handgun was hers. It was a 9 mm thankfully. She'd had the most experience with that kind.

She almost laughed out loud. All of her experience had been gained in the past week, amounted to simple target practice, and had been accomplished with Logan as her teacher. Fat lot of good it had done her yesterday. She couldn't have killed that guard when Esteban ordered her to if her life had depended upon it. Probably it had, but she'd wiggled her way out of that one...barely.

Now all she had to do was survive this little errand for the boss.

Logan stepped out of the bedroom in a pair of tight black jeans and matching T-shirt. Though his hair was still damp he looked good enough to eat.

Oh, yeah, this morning's job was the least of her worries. Not losing her heart to Logan was going to be the biggest test of all.

"You hungry?" he asked in that deep, resonant voice that made her shiver. "I'm starved."

She was hungry all right, but it had nothing to do with food.

A CARGO PLANE, somewhat larger and a great deal less luxurious than the one in which she and Logan had arrived in Colombia, took them to a small airstrip near Ciudad Acuna, Mexico, a stone's throw from the Texas border. Dumb as a post, Hector Caldarone turned out to be a pretty good pilot considering what he had to work with. There was only one point where Erin thought she might lose the breakfast she'd hastily wolfed down that morning. But things had settled down once the aircraft had skidded to a halt.

On the ground there wasn't much to see outside the primitive airstrip and the waiting SUVs. A panel van sporting the logo of a well-known courier service arrived shortly after they landed. Four armed men stood silently by, most likely awaiting instructions. The Caldarone brothers spoke quietly to one of the men while several of the others hurriedly hid the plane in a dilapidated barn-turned-warehouse nearby. The group was then separated into three teams. She and Logan would ride with Hector and Carlos. Two of the men would stay behind to guard the plane, while the others climbed into the remaining vehicles.

A short time later, they were in position. According to Carlos's briefing, the truck was headed to the military's newest training center in an undisclosed area of southern Texas. The weapons they carried were a new prototype that would make the M16 and its subsequent upgrades obsolete.

This information meant little to Erin other than it was probably dangerous. It amazed her that she was standing here, beneath the scorching Texas sun waiting for a load of military weapons to arrive so she could help steal them.

The reality erupted inside her like a train exploding from a dark tunnel. She could be killed in the next few minutes. People who stole things—especially weapons—were, more often than not, shot at. She didn't know how to do any of this. She was just a computer security analyst with too much *time* on her hands. One who'd been tricked into breaking the law. Just look where that momentary stupidity had gotten her.

Laughter bubbled into her throat. This was insane. She turned to Logan and almost said as much... *almost.* She opened her mouth and nothing came out. Her heart slammed so mercilessly against her sternum that she simply could not speak. Yet he looked as cool as the proverbial cucumber.

She could *not* do this.

No way.

She didn't belong here.

Trouble. Logan saw it in Bailey's eyes. He'd seen that look one other time and she'd gone postal on him then. He glanced furtively at the other men lounging patiently near their vehicles. This was not a good time for her to lose it. His gaze landed back on hers at the same time her hand went slack and the weapon there dropped to the ground.

Damn.

If anyone noticed... He did the only thing he could. He grabbed her by the shoulders and kissed her. Kissed her hard. She whimpered at first and shoved against his chest, but he just kissed her that much harder. Forcing her lips apart and invading the sweet, hot territory beyond. A new kind of tension zipped through him, hardening every muscle that wasn't already on red alert. Her mouth softened beneath his and he eased off on the pressure, allowing the kiss to evolve into something else...something that had nothing to do with shutting her up.

The men laughed and made lewd remarks, but otherwise didn't pay the two of them more than passing notice.

Fire heated Logan's loins, racing through his limbs, making him want to drag her down to the sand and—

Damn.

He pulled back. Set her away from him.

He'd almost lost all perspective there. It was bad enough one of them already had.

She blinked to banish the haze of lust from her eyes. As he held her gaze he pressed one finger to her lips and shook his head ever so slightly. He hoped like hell she understood that this was definitely not the time to lose it. Most of these guys were the trigger-happy types. It wouldn't take much to send any one of them on a shooting rampage.

She drew in a ragged breath, then bent down and retrieved her weapon. When she'd straightened, folded her arms over her chest and leaned against the SUV as if all were well, he finally took a breath.

Close.

Too close.

Twenty minutes passed with no contact from the rest of the ground support team. Hector Caldarone had started to pace restlessly.

Logan braced himself for the worst. Any time a job went sour, bad things happened.

"Something is wrong," Hector announced the obvious.

Carlos muttered something inaudible in Spanish.

"The truck will come," Jose, the apparent leader of the ground support team, urged. "You will see." He nodded adamantly. "It will come."

As he studied Jose's body language, the hair on the back of Logan's neck suddenly stood on end. The guy was one of the group who'd arrived in the panel van. He was entirely too agitated. Yet he insisted that all was as it should be, as if he were trying to convince himself, as well as those around him. He knew something.

Hector swore heatedly as he continued to pace. This was his run. Logan was certain he didn't want anything to go wrong. Esteban would likely hold him personally responsible.

Instinct still nagging at him, Logan took a few steps toward the panel van, as if he, too, intended to pace out his impatience. When he reached the overly enthusiastic Jose, their gazes locked. Logan saw the truth he couldn't hide in the man's eyes. In one rapid motion, Logan pivoted and pressed the barrel of his weapon to Jose's forehead.

"What is it you're not telling us, *amigo?*"

The click of weapons engaging echoed behind him. Logan ignored it.

"What the hell are you doing?" Hector demanded.

"This guy knows something's up," Logan explained, his gaze never leaving Jose's terror filled eyes. Oh, yeah, this guy was scared. He knew something big. "It's a setup, isn't it?" Logan suggested. "Maybe that truck isn't even coming. Or maybe we're sitting ducks."

"It's coming! It's coming! I swear it!" Jose cried.

"Don't move!"

The command came from Bailey somewhere behind Logan. He tensed. That couldn't be good, he estimated with mushrooming dread. He glanced over his shoulder and his heart stalled in his chest.

Damn.

She'd stepped between him and one of the other

guys from the panel van. She held her weapon in both hands aimed right in the guy's face. Logan swore again.

"What is *this?*" Hector shouted, desperation making his voice too high-pitched.

Carlos threw up his hands and cursed everyone present and then their mothers, respectively. "Just shoot them," he insisted impatiently. "Esteban will kill us all anyway!"

"I'm telling you, Hector," Bailey cut in. "Logan knows what he's talking about. He can feel these things," she added.

Smooth, Logan admitted. Very smooth.

"You'd better do something," Bailey urged when no one acted on her suggestion. "We may not have much time."

Logan tossed Jose's weapon away. "I'd listen to her if I were you, Hector." Logan stared straight into the eyes of the man at the business end of his weapon. "We've been had."

Five seconds turned into ten and nobody moved. Logan shoved his prisoner toward Carlos. "Just ask him nicely and see if I'm right." Logan turned immediately to Bailey and quickly took charge of the guy she had under a bead. Logan glared at her. She frowned, then shrugged as if to say, "What'd I do?" When this was over...

He shook his head. If either of them lived long enough to call it over, it would be no small miracle.

The interrogation that followed took only about five minutes. Ten minutes after that the hijacked truck arrived, driven by friends of the two dead men hidden behind the panel van. The two newcomers quickly joined their friends. The crates of weapons were swiftly transferred to the panel van. The traitors were left for nature and the environment to take care of cleanup detail.

The two men who guarded the plane suffered the same fate as the other traitors.

Logan didn't breathe easy until the weapons were loaded onto the aircraft and they were back in the air. Esteban would not be happy that his supposedly loyal supporter in Texas had turned traitor on him. According to the man Hector had questioned, his boss had decided to hijack the weapons for another buyer. One thing that could be counted on, Esteban would not rest until he'd settled this nasty business with his man in Texas. Logan wondered if the traitor knew he was dead already.

Right now, Logan had his own problems. He glanced at Bailey. He wasn't happy with her at all. She'd taken a hell of a risk jumping into the middle of a tense situation like that. What could she have been thinking? She wasn't trained for that sort of thing. Hell, she barely knew how to fire a weapon much less make a move like that. He clenched his jaw to keep from ranting at her now.

It would have to wait until they could talk…which might not be any time soon.

ERIN WAS PRETTY SURE she'd never seen anyone get as angry as Esteban had. She reached into the shower and twisted the knobs allowing the water time to heat up while she undressed. She checked her ugly bruise in the mirror. The lump was pretty much gone, but her temple and part of her cheek looked absolutely awful and was immensely tender.

She studied her reflection a moment longer. She'd done good today. Even after almost losing it at first, she'd stopped that guy from jumping Logan, killing him probably. Pride welled in her chest. That's right. She'd most likely saved the ungrateful jerk's life, and he'd been upset with her since. She couldn't figure it out. Hector and Carlos thought she was *muy bueno!* But Logan treated her like a refugee from the enemy camp.

What did it take to please the man?

The memory of that bare chest and how it had felt to be locked in those strong arms practically melted her. And that kiss he'd laid on her today!—it was all that had saved her from going schizoid.

She might not ever know what pleased Logan, but she definitely knew what tripped her trigger—he did.

She sighed and glared into the mirror in self-disgust. What a mess. She couldn't do anything right. *If* she lived through this mission she would never see Logan again. She stared at the tiny gold band on her hand. None of this was real. Not even the strength and courage she'd suddenly possessed when she thought Logan's life was in danger.

It was all make-believe…pretend. They were both just playing their part. Very soon it would be over one way or another.

No point fretting over it, she decided as she kicked off her sneakers and reached for the snap of her jeans. It wouldn't be the first time she'd fallen for the wrong guy. She sighed again. But why did this suddenly feel like the only one that counted?

The bathroom door burst open and Logan barged in.

"I'm taking a shower," she snapped, whirling to face him and suddenly feeling as if she'd somehow inadvertently telegraphed her previous thoughts to him. The way he looked made her shiver. Color heated her cheeks.

"So am I," he growled.

Her eyes rounded in surprise, her mouth dropped open, but before she could demand an explanation, he grabbed her and backed her into the shower. The moment they were both fully inside he closed the door and glared down at her.

The hot water sprayed down on them like a thousand tiny needles, plastering their shirts to their bodies. Steam billowed, adding another layer of tension. When she regained her senses and would have yelled at him, one strong hand clamped over her mouth.

He pressed his lips against her ear and whispered, "Don't make a sound. Just listen."

Fear surged through her. Had something happened? Had their covers been blown? If they tried to run, where could they go? Her heart lurched. *Oh damn.* And here she'd thought they'd saved the day...earned a little of Esteban's respect.

"Don't ever do anything as stupid as what you did

today again. Do you understand me?'' he murmured, his voice harsh, impatient.

He drew back and glowered down at her. Frowning her confusion, she shook her head to indicate that she didn't understand.

His lips brushed the shell of her ear once more. ''That man could have killed you,'' he growled savagely. ''You're not trained for that kind of exchange. From now on you stay in the background. Got it?''

Fury ignited inside her, burning away the fear she'd felt only moments before. When he would have drawn back she gripped him by the shoulders and jerked him back to her. She told him in no uncertain terms where he could go and what he could do when he got there. *''Comprende?''* she muttered tightly, then shoved the door open in invitation for him to get the hell out of her shower.

The staring contest lasted less than ten seconds. He stormed out of the glass cubicle, wet black cotton molding to every perfect contour of that awesome body. Swearing silently, Erin leaned back against the slick wall and closed her eyes. He slammed the door behind him. Glass rattled. She jumped then forced a couple more slow, deep breaths as the hot water continued to shower down on her. She really was an idiot. She had risked her life for the jerk and he had the nerve to dash it in her face.

Muttering every curse word she knew and some she'd only heard the guards around here use, she peeled off her soaked clothes, tossed them out the door, and continued with her shower. Maybe if she took her time she'd use up all the hot water. That thought brought a smile to her lips. A cold shower would be good for a hothead like Logan.

Later, when she'd once more put off the inevitable until the last possible minute, she climbed into bed with him. She kept as close to the edge and as far away as possible. She might have to sleep with him, but she didn't have to get close to him...she didn't even have to like it.

Sadly though, she did like it.

She could hear him breathing—slow, steady breaths. She could smell his masculine scent. Unfortunately she could remember all too well how it felt to be in his arms.

Erin squeezed her eyes shut and forced all thoughts of Logan from her mind. All she had to do was go to sleep then she wouldn't have to think. But she would dream...

Her eyes popped open wide.

She was screwed.

There was no escape.

In one way or another, she'd been just as much a prisoner since entering Logan's custody as she had been in the penitentiary.

Nothing had changed.

No, that wasn't right.

Everything had changed.

Chapter Eight

"Three days," Esteban reiterated. "It has been three days since the traitor tried to steal my weapons and still he has not been found."

Logan waited patiently for him to go on. He'd been raving for the past half hour without really saying anything at all. He paced back and forth behind his elegant mahogany desk and blew off steam about how he couldn't find his former business associate in Texas. Logan wasn't even sure why he was here, in Esteban's private office, listening to his tirade and watching him wear a hole in the expensive carpet.

"You." Esteban stopped his incessant pacing and stabbed a finger in Logan's direction. "You were the only one who sensed something was wrong. Hector or Carlos should have noticed the man's agitation." He shook his head. "There is no excuse."

"I was closer to him," Logan offered.

Esteban shook his head. "That is no excuse. Your instincts are better, that is the answer. I think perhaps the Caldarone brothers have become lax in their attitudes."

Was this an opportunity for advancement, Logan wondered. If so, he'd take it. He'd learned nothing of value since their arrival. Esteban was far too tight-lipped even with his most trusted personnel to reveal his sources and, so far, getting near his personal computer was a bust. Logan needed to complete this mission—pronto. Erin Bailey was driving him absolutely crazy. If he had to spend one more night in that bed with her and without touching her...

He couldn't think about that right now. He had to stay focused. Esteban was staring at him with an intensity that bordered on lunacy.

"I need new blood in key positions," Esteban was saying. He halted abruptly and braced his hands on his desktop and leaned forward. "Like you, my new friend."

Logan shrugged. "I'm ready to do whatever you need me to. Just name it."

Esteban studied him closer still. "I believe you are." Something changed in his eyes. "And your wife, she is a valuable asset as well."

"To *me,* she is," Logan said pointedly.

Esteban straightened and stroked his chin thoughtfully. "Yes, yes. Loyalty is of the utmost importance. Without loyalty a man—or woman," he amended, "is nothing. You cannot be truly loyal and become so lax in your duties."

"I agree." Logan forced his posture to relax since Esteban had moved his focus beyond Bailey. Now was not the time for a display of possessiveness toward his undercover wife, Logan realized. He'd acted foolishly enough three days ago after the run to Texas. Bailey had barely spoken to him since.

Esteban sat down on the edge of his desk. "There is a very important job coming up in a couple of days. I would like you and your lovely wife to take the lead."

Logan sat up straighter, feigning an exaggerated enthusiasm. "We'll be ready."

Esteban nodded. "Good. I will have the details worked out soon."

Logan started to get up, but Esteban delayed him with a wave of his hand. "There is one thing more."

Going on immediate alert, Logan eased back down into his chair. "That would be?"

Esteban tapped his chin and released a heavy breath. "You and your wife appear to work together quite well. I am very impressed with all that I have seen." His brow furrowed. "But is everything okay personally? Is the honeymoon over already?"

Realization struck Logan instantly. Of course he'd known their apartment would be monitored. He'd been so concerned about what they said and did that he hadn't considered what they *didn't* say and do.

"Is there a problem?" Esteban suggested.

Well, that was just great. Apparently Logan's epiphany had also been written all over his face. "No." He flared his hands. "The opportunity to join your family has been a major change for us." He lifted one shoulder in a shrug. "We've led a rather free lifestyle and this is definitely a radical about-face." Logan manufactured a sincere smile. "But we're adapting."

Esteban acknowledged his explanation with a nod. "I can see how such a change would cause a *temporary* setback. Well, then." He stood. Logan followed suit. "I will trust that things are okay."

"Count on it," Logan allowed graciously. "I look forward to the upcoming opportunity you mentioned. We won't disappoint you."

"I am sure you won't."

Logan left Esteban's private office. He had absolutely no idea how he was going to pull this off. As much as he wanted her, he couldn't…no, he wouldn't ask Bailey to have sex with him just to please Esteban.

There had to be another way.

ERIN SLOWED to a fast walk as she rounded the back corner of the main house. She was breathing hard and sweating pretty heavily from her run. With the difference in altitude she couldn't quite make her usual number of miles, but she wanted to stay in shape. Just in case she had to run like hell to save her hide before this was over.

God, would it ever be over?

Things between her and Logan were so tense now that being in the same room together was like skating on thin ice. One never knew when it was going to crack. They scarcely spoke except when necessary to maintain their cover. They barely even looked at each other.

But the nights were the worst. Lying in bed next to each other. Wanting…needing, but unable to even bear touching. It was truly miserable. If she dreamed of Logan's making love to her once more, she might just explode! Or jump his bones when he least expected it.

Erin expelled a weary breath. She just didn't know what to make of this crazy physical attraction. Logan was like the enemy really. Sure he was the good guy and was going to help her get her freedom back...but he was the one who'd gotten her into this mess. So, in effect, he was the enemy.

And she was sleeping with him.

What was worse she wanted to have sex with him almost as much as she wanted her freedom back.

Okay, maybe that was an exaggeration, but it wasn't far off base.

"Well, well, if it isn't Miss Athletic."

Erin resisted the urge to roll her eyes at the sound of Sheila's annoying voice. Instead, she forced a smile and said, "Hello, Sheila." In this new nightmare she'd signed on for, Sheila was the bane of Erin's existence. A real pain in the behind. "Still contaminating your lungs with those cigarettes I see."

The woman was out of her chair and in Erin's face before she could gloat over her own wittiness.

"You'd better be careful," Sheila warned. She waved her cigarette close to Erin's face. "I can make things pretty hot for you."

Not really afraid, but too smart not to be a little nervous around the woman, Erin held up her hands. "Just kidding. Just kidding." Sheila really hated her. Erin was pretty sure it had something to do with Esteban's obvious interest in her.

Sheila glowered. Her ruby red lips curled in anger. "I warned you to remember your place and somehow you just keep forgetting. This is my final warning. Next time—"

"Mrs. Watters."

The feminine voice came from somewhere beyond the terrace. Sheila and Erin both spun in that direction. To Erin's disbelief, Esteban's sister stepped from beneath the cover of the shaded terrace.

"I would like to speak with Mrs. Wilks privately," she said, her voice serene, regal, just like the rest of her.

Sheila blinked, disbelief instantly defusing her fury. "Of course." She slinked away without even a final glare in Erin's direction.

Erin, too, was in a mild state of shock at the moment. Maria had never uttered a single syllable in Erin's presence or anyone else's as far as she could tell. Everyone pretended she wasn't there. Esteban appeared to want it that way. It seemed to Erin that he treated her rather subserviently, rarely even introducing her.

"You are available to walk with me for a time, yes?"

A newly born cynicism gave Erin pause. Was this a trick question? Was she only going to get into more trouble with Logan if she said yes? Or if she didn't, would Esteban simply kill her for giving his only sibling the brush-off? Then again, she'd love to know more about this quietly elegant lady. After all, she was in the spy business now.

Curiosity got the better of her.

"Sure. I've got plenty of time." She mopped her brow with the back of her hand and suddenly hoped she didn't smell to high heaven. She was sweating like a pitcher during the last seconds of the final inning of the game, bases loaded and only one strike to go to win. The outcome could go either way. Not unlike Erin's own situation.

Maria turned and started in the direction of the garden. At least Erin had been told there was a garden beyond the privacy fence. No one was allowed inside.

The six-foot tall stone wall that served as the fence was covered in ivy and had only one entrance as far as she could tell. An extra wide, arched wooden door and formidable looking lock kept those as curious as Erin out. She'd decided that it most likely hid a torture chamber for Esteban's pleasure rather than a garden as she'd been told. Why would anyone keep a garden locked?

Now she knew. It was for his sister's pleasure and he allowed no fraternization with his sister.

Maria unlocked the heavy door and led the way. She closed it as soon as Erin was inside.

"This is my first love," she explained.

Erin could only stare, openmouthed, at the lush, lovely garden. Roses she recognized, most of the rest were foreign to her…probably indigenous to the area. Then again, she'd never had a green thumb. She'd spent all her time inside an office with only a widescreen computer monitor and the World Wide Web to keep her company.

"It's breathtaking." Erin bent to smell the nearest rose, a deep crimson red.

"Those are my favorite." Maria snapped off a long stem and offered the lush flower to Erin. "This variety is superb in many ways, color, size, fragrance, but it is even more special than an admirer first suspects."

Erin took the rose gingerly, hoping to avoid the thorns. To her surprise there were none.

Maria smiled. "The lack of thorns makes the rose perfect. Its beauty is not marred by the threat of violence."

Interesting. Erin decided the flower was very much like the woman who tended it, beautiful and completely harmless. Such an unexpected thing to find in this world of treachery and murder.

"I didn't know this kind existed," Erin admitted. Truth was she knew nothing at all about roses except that she liked to get them from a guy.

"I deplore violence of any sort," Maria offered as she began to walk.

Erin followed, dividing her focus between the beautifully vivid scenery and the unexpectedly fascinating woman. "I guess that makes life here difficult for you."

Silence.

Erin wanted to bite off her tongue. Why the hell had she said that? Hell's bells, was she nuts? There was no way the statement could be taken any way except negative toward the woman's brother.

Maria looked at her, her black eyes clear, unaccusing. "I find it very difficult."

Relief, so profound that her knees almost buckled beneath her, rushed through Erin. "I didn't mean that in a bad way." Right! Another lame remark.

The woman smiled. "I know you did not. You are not like the rest. I…" She seemed to search for the right word. "I *feel* no malice in you."

Erin's pulse rate picked up. This could be good or bad, depending upon how one looked at it. The last thing she needed was this nice lady blowing her cover. "Well, I can't claim I'm innocent."

Maria continued forward, her gaze now on the path before them that wove through the rows of exquisite flowers. "Yes, but you are different from the others. I realized that when you refused to kill Manuel as my brother suggested."

Damn. Erin knew that little episode was going to come back to bite her in the butt. "I couldn't kill him for my own mistake," she hurriedly explained. "The whole thing was my fault."

"Few would have admitted that truth. My brother was correct." She settled that serene gaze on Erin once more. "You are a very brave woman."

Enough talk about her, Erin decided, far too nervous about where this might be headed. "So, how long have you lived here?" she asked, injecting a casualness she didn't feel into her tone.

"Pablo made this our home ten years ago."

Ten years. Had Maria never been married? Never had a life of her own away from her brother. "You're not married?"

Another moment of silence.

Okay, so she'd stuck her big foot in her mouth again. She'd just about gotten used to the taste of shoe leather.

"No," Maria said finally. "I have never been married. I leave home only to purchase new varieties for my garden. And even then Pablo worries himself sick until I am safely home again."

In other words, she had no life outside the domain of her brother. She was a prisoner...just like Erin.

She had to ask. Fear of making a mistake pounded in her brain, but she ignored it. She had to know. "Do you ever resent him being so overprotective?"

Maria paused and looked directly into Erin's eyes. "At times, but he loves me and has only my best interest at heart." She looked to the north, seemingly far beyond the stone fence that defined this small, fiercely guarded space of hers. "It is a very cruel world. Very little is sacred. It is a constant battle for my dear brother. He works far too hard."

Erin could only nod, pretending to agree. Old Pablo had this woman completely fooled. She thought he was only protecting her by keeping her locked away here. Worst of all, she believed him to be some sort of hardworking businessman. Erin resisted the impulse to ask her if she knew precisely how her brother earned his living. Thankfully, good sense prevailed and she kept her mouth shut.

Maria started back toward the entrance. "We must talk again soon, Sara. May I call you Sara?"

"Of course." Erin manufactured a smile. "Thank you for sharing your lovely garden with me."

"It was my pleasure."

Erin headed in the direction of the guest house, her mind still reeling with what she'd learned about Esteban's sister. But the truly scary part was that Maria had hit the nail on the head where Erin was concerned. She wasn't like the others.

She'd have to find a way to remedy that, but first she had to take a shower.

LOGAN HAD SPENT an hour with Larry Watters and the Caldarone brothers going over the final shipment orders for the weapons they'd stolen three days ago. The one thing Logan did have at this point was a customer list with half a dozen names on it. A few he'd recognized, the rest were new to him.

Mission Recovery would get the scoop on all concerned as soon as Logan was able to get the list to Ferrelli. As the assigned guardian angel, Ferrelli would be in-country somewhere. He would be watching Logan's every move, when he had the opportunity to make contact he would and Logan would give him the intelligence report.

He heard the muffled sound of water spraying as soon as he entered their quarters. Logan locked the door behind him and headed that way. He knew what he had to do and there was simply no way around it. Esteban was already suspicious.

The room was hot and steamy. Erin's running clothes lay on the floor, her shoes kicked carelessly aside. She was humming something. Slightly off-key. A smile kicked up one corner of his mouth. That was just one of the little things about her that got to him. He tried to fight it, but it was useless.

He reached for the door, his gaze riveted to the silhouette behind the foggy glass. Studying the barely visible feminine curves of her body was all it took to finish him off. Arousal was instantaneous. He clenched his jaw and told himself again that he had to do this. The mission had to be top priority and their cover was essential to the success of the mission.

The realization that he was fully clothed made him hesitate. He wasn't about to get into that shower again with his clothes on. Been there, done that. He quickly discarded his shoes and clothes, tossing them next to the others already on the floor. This time when he reached for the door he didn't hesitate. He opened it and stepped inside.

In the middle of rinsing the shampoo from her hair, Erin's eyes flew open and she squealed. "What the—?"

Logan closed his mouth over hers. His arms went around her and he pulled her close, forcing her to acknowledge the intimacy of their nude bodies. She pushed against his chest, squirmed in his arms, but he stilled her with his kiss. He plundered and stroked until she felt boneless against him and whimpered in surrender. Only then did he dare take his mouth from hers.

"Esteban is listening," he murmured against the shell of her ear. "He's suspicious because we're not having a physical relationship."

She gasped and attempted to draw away from him once more.

"We have to make this sound real," he urged. "Trust me. I won't..." This would be the difficult part. "I won't let things go too far. You have my word."

She hesitated, then nodded.

He drew back, his gaze immediately roving her body. He couldn't help it...he had to see. She pushed the hair back from her eyes and did the same. He didn't miss the answering spark of desire in her eyes.

Logan turned off the water and led Erin from the shower. He grabbed the fluffy towel waiting on the rack and dried her skin. He rubbed gently, teasing her skin, her nipples with the thick terry cloth. Her breathing grew more rapid, more uneven. His own did the same. He focused on the task, rather than the woman, his body already way past aroused.

He knelt and dragged the towel down each toned thigh and calf. He kept his attention carefully diverted from the wedge of silky blond hair between her thighs. He reminded himself that this was part of the job...necessary to the mission. When she turned for him, he gave the same treatment to her backside. The gentle swell of her buttocks almost snapped his control, but he fought the need pounding in his veins.

It wasn't until she'd taken the towel and begun to dry him that he was convinced he would never survive this encounter without going too far. And he'd promised...

He led her to the bed and ushered her onto it. Whatever happened next it had to at least sound real. He lay down beside her and those big innocent eyes went even wider with uncertainty.

"Take it easy, Baby. Just let me show you how much you mean to me."

He kissed her again, laved her lips, the innermost recesses of her mouth. Her fingers splayed over his chest, restraining, yet at the same time unwittingly encouraging. His arousal nudged her thigh. She moaned softly and her nails bit into his skin. Driven by the fever raging inside him, he kissed her chin, down the length of her creamy throat, then lower. When he reached her breasts, he traced the smooth globe with his tongue. Every instinct warned him that this was going too far…but nothing short of sudden death was going to stop him.

She moaned louder. Her hands went to his shoulders, pushing him away, but he would not relent. He took one pebbled peak into his mouth and suckled it. She cried out, her fingers clutching now rather than repelling.

He teased her firm nipples, tugged and suckled each until she writhed beneath him, then he moved lower. He kissed his way down her rib cage, dipped his tongue into her belly button.

"Oh, Logan!" Her hips undulated, reaching for him, for the relief she sought. Her eyes were clenched tightly shut. Her face a study in fierce concentration.

He lifted her hips and nuzzled her mound. She screamed, arching against him. He thrust his tongue inside, tasted her, withdrew, then suckled until she screamed again. He plunged with his tongue, with his fingers, tasted, teased, sucked until her feminine muscles clenched and the spasms of release began. Her body stiffened, then went limp as one final cry of ecstasy trembled past her lips.

His heart thundered in his chest, his body was taut, on the edge. He wanted to thrust into her so badly he groaned savagely with restraint. His closest encounter with death had not caused him more pain than this! He panted with the effort of calming his body. Every muscle throbbed, wanting, needing. His fingers fisted in the covers as he pushed himself fully away from her sweet body.

Cool fingers suddenly encircled him...he gasped, his eyes closing with the unbearable pleasure of it. She moved, tugged at the flesh of his painfully erect sex. Another savage roar tore from his throat. He wanted to resist her ministrations, but he couldn't. He needed this too much. His entire body tautened to the point of snapping.

Her movements, at first gentle, then growing desperate, she quickly brought him to release. His body arched upward, he uttered a sound that was more growl than groan as she pumped the last remnants of completion from him.

The unexpected satiation only made him feel more desperate, but he forced himself to relax fully into the thick covers. Their ragged breathing was the only sound in the room. The scent of sex cloaked them, held them in a fragile spell. He wanted to say something—to somehow make it...less crude than it had been. But there was nothing to say. It had all been an act of desperation...for Esteban's ears. They were only helpless players, trying to stay alive.

She rolled away from him, shattering the moment, and rushed to the bathroom, closing the door behind her. Logan closed his eyes and for the first time in his career hated himself...hated what he did.

But he had no choice.

She had no choice.

Chapter Nine

Saturday morning brought a whole new onslaught of concerns and worries for Erin. She supposed that she should be thankful that she had survived five days and nights as Esteban's guest. Somehow, she wasn't.

Erin dropped onto the foot of the bed, drew up one leg and tied her sneaker. Let's see, she'd been physically assaulted by an overenthusiastic guard, she'd survived two up-close encounters with Sheila, who seemed to have it in for her for no real reason, Esteban made her increasingly nervous for more reasons than one...

And she'd had almost-sex with Logan.

She rested her head on her knee and sighed.

What a fool she was.

She blew out another breath as she dropped her foot to the floor, lifted the other and tied the remaining sneaker. It wouldn't have been nearly so bad if she hadn't acted like a sex-starved nympho at his first touch. God, she'd survived a crash course in Spy 101 and Remedial Weaponry, but she was pretty sure her heart would never survive Advanced John Logan.

When she'd awakened this morning she'd been immensely grateful that Logan was gone already. She wasn't sure she could face him anytime soon. Maybe not even in this lifetime.

They didn't have another job until Monday. Maybe she could find a way to avoid him the entire weekend. Maria might be interested in giving her another tour of the garden. Or maybe she and Sheila could exchange recipes.

Yeah, right.

The only thing Sheila wanted from Erin was possibly a couple of vital organs, starting with her heart or maybe a lung.

She supposed she could always join the guards in one of their card games. They were all afraid of her now that she was Esteban's newest pet. She stood and combed her fingers through her hair. At least all that ogling she endured from him paid off.

Maria sounded like the best bet for a few hours of distraction. Erin headed for the door. Maybe she'd take up gardening herself if she ever got back home.

Home. Atlanta felt a million miles away right now. Too far away to even think about.

The door opened just as she reached it.

Logan.

She clamped down on her lower lip to hold back the curse that rushed to the tip of her tongue. Dammit, why hadn't she moved a little faster? Then she could have avoided this seriously awkward confrontation.

And why did he have to look so damned good? Her greedy gaze perused his body in one continuous sweep. Snug jeans...body-molding, worn-thin cotton shirt with the top two buttons opened. She swallowed hard. As if the masculine frame wasn't enough to completely disarm a woman, there was that gorgeous face. She wasn't even going into the eyes, the hair or the perfect cut of his nose and that marvelously chiseled jaw.

"Grab your purse," he said nonchalantly, as if she hadn't just sized him up like the best cut of beef in the market. "We're taking a little trip into town."

She shrugged her shoulders and displayed her palms in the universal gesture of confusion.

He touched one finger to his lips, then said, "I thought it was time I took my Baby shopping for a new dress. Especially since there's going to be a party tomorrow evening."

She looked surprised. "A party? That's...great!" She backed toward the table where her purse lay. "Wow! What a treat." She slung her purse over her shoulder. "It's been weeks since you took me shopping. I can't wait. And a party!"

Glowering, he sliced a hand through the air letting her know that was enough.

She glared right back. How did she know when enough was enough? All this cloak-and-dagger crap was new to her.

Wow...she slowed as she started back toward the door. A revelation struck her like a bolt of unexpected summer lightning. She was a true-to-life spy.

Wasn't that something?

She frowned at her spy partner as she sidled past him and out the door. Wasn't this fun? Just like a Mission Impossible flick.

SHE WAS STILL ANGRY with him about yesterday.

Logan blew out a disgusted breath and trailed after Erin.

He swore. When the hell had he started thinking of her as Erin? Right before he'd made her come for the first time, he admitted ruefully.

Medellín was a busy place on Saturday, he noted, trying his level best to keep his attention off the swaying derriere in front of him. He was glad for the reprieve. The tension was getting to both of them. A little time away from *work* would do them good. Besides, they needed to talk and doing it in the shower wasn't going to work anymore. When he stood beneath that hot spray now all he could think about was how it felt to touch Erin…to taste her.

"Logan."

He stopped just short of running right into her. "What?" he demanded, dragging his attention back to the present.

"How much money did you say you had?"

He rolled his eyes, not that she could see since he was wearing dark glasses. "Enough."

She smiled and shoved the two bags she carried already at him. "Good. I'm sure I'll find a few more things I need."

Now how the hell was he supposed to be ready to protect her life if his hands were full of frigging shopping bags?

A long, slow whistle jerked his attention forward. A guy leaning against the wall up ahead was eyeing Erin—Bailey, dammit.

Despite the dark glasses and the baseball cap with its concealing brim pulled down low over his face, Logan recognized him.

Ferrelli. His guardian angel.

Bailey turned and gifted Ferrelli with a wide, flirty smile.

"Oh, honey, make my day," Ferrelli offered in that exaggerated Italian accent he only used when he really needed it or wanted to impress the ladies.

"Sorry, buddy," Bailey said as she kept right on walking. She hitched a thumb over her shoulder. "I already have a sugar daddy."

Logan steamed when he noted the extra inspiration in her walk. For Ferrelli's benefit no doubt. He wondered what she'd think when she found out she'd just flirted with their only contact between here and a safe zone.

Catching up to her, Logan passed the shopping bag in his right hand to his left and slung his arm around her shoulders. "How about some lunch, Baby?"

She lifted a finely arched eyebrow above her own designer shades. "Only if you promise to take me to that clothing boutique over there before we leave town."

He glanced in the direction she indicated and groaned. Only the ritziest place in the whole city. He bared his teeth in a feral smile. "Sure, Baby, anything you want."

To her obvious consternation, he picked the restaurant and ordered for both of them. They ate slowly, relishing the cuisine, speaking only occasionally.

He'd watched her all morning. She'd been so animated. He'd never seen her like that. She loved the colors, the textures of the fabrics, everything. Her Spanish was pretty good. The way she moved was—he caught himself before he sighed—amazing. She'd proven to be a pretty amazing woman all the way around. He wondered if she realized just how amazing she really was.

"You're not eating," she noted, wading into his reverie.

"I'm thinking," he said honestly. About you, he didn't add.

"Ooow, that's scary," she teased before taking a long drink of her white wine.

Yeah, he agreed silently, it is. This woman was so far under his skin that it was definitely scary.

It was crazy, that's what it was. They had nothing in common. As soon as this mission was over, assuming they survived it, she'd be out of his life. And even if by some strange stroke of fate they made a mutual decision to see where this thing between them went, well that would be over just as soon as she realized the truth.

Lucas or Casey, or maybe both, had set her up. They'd set things in motion, the prison guard, the inmate, to make her more receptive to their offer if they ever needed her particular skills. And they had the evidence to clear her.

She would hold that against Logan if she learned the truth. And this thing between them couldn't go any further without complete honesty. He wouldn't allow it.

She would have to know and that would be the end of it.

He looked away from her. Why did that idea suddenly seem like the worst thing that could happen in his life? He'd been in dozens of relationships in the past, always intense, but brief. But there was something different this time. Something he couldn't put his finger on. Maybe her vulnerability made him more protective of her. Whatever it was, it was powerful. He'd have to watch his step here or he'd be in over his head.

Noting that Erin was about to devour the last bite of her dessert, Logan took the napkin from beneath his drink and scribbled the list of names on it. This might be the only opportunity he'd have to get the intelligence to Lucas. Mission Recovery needed to know where the stolen weapons were going. Logan wadded the napkin and placed it next to his glass.

"Finished?" he asked Erin.

She nodded. "Stuffed." She closed her eyes and moaned with satisfaction as she swallowed the last sip of the expensive wine. "Thank you," she purred.

Logan's mouth went instantly dry when she licked her lips slowly, seductively. Other parts of him reacted as well.

He dropped some cash onto the table, pushed to his feet, then stepped around to pull out her chair. "I'm glad you enjoyed it."

"If I'm going to need a dress, does that mean you'll need a suit?"

He ignored her question even though she was right. Esteban wanted all his people looking good tomorrow night for his impromptu shindig.

Near the double entry doors, Logan paused as if searching for something in his pockets. He watched as the waitress cleared their table. As she passed Ferrelli, sitting two tables over, he snagged her wrist and spoke to her. When she leaned closer to answer him, he retrieved the wadded napkin from the tray she carried without missing a beat.

Satisfied, Logan opened the door for Erin and ushered her out onto the crowded street. The list would be in Lucas's possession within the hour. Now if Erin could just get into Esteban's private office and shake down his personal computer. It was the only hope for nailing the bastard since Esteban never personally conducted any of the business transactions himself. And no one they'd caught dared to rat on him. Not even one telephone call or electronic transmission had ever connected Esteban to his illegal trade. Erin was their only hope of nailing him and his contact.

Logan had a bad feeling that accomplishing that feat was going to carry a higher price tag than Erin would want to pay…than he would want her to pay.

Just another warning that this thing between them had gotten out of hand.

Time to take a step back.

NO SOONER had they returned to the estate, than Logan was whisked away by Watters and the still depressed

Caldarone brothers. Both looked as if they'd been on a three-day drinking binge. Erin decided to pay that visit to Maria now. Sitting around their quarters or lounging on the terrace with Sheila held no appeal whatsoever.

And she had to do something to keep her mind off Logan.

Maybe she'd get lucky and the men folk would disappear for a few hours and then she could have the run of the house.

Yeah, right, like that was going to happen.

Erin waltzed into the big old hacienda as if she owned the place. And why not? She knew her way around the parlor and dining room. Had even been to the briefing room just down the hall. All she had to do was ask one of the guards hanging around inside where she might find Maria.

Well, what do you know? The guy, Manuel, who owed her a favor was stationed right where the long entry hall forked into the east and west wings of the downstairs portion of the massive house.

"Hola," she ventured.

Manuel studied her for a moment, then muttered, *"Hola."*

"I'm looking for, Maria." She tucked her fingers into the back pockets of her jeans. "I wanted to talk to her about her flowers."

"She is not here."

A frown tugged at Erin's forehead. "Oh." That was odd. Maria talked as if she rarely left the place. *"Gracias."*

Manuel grunted something inaudible.

Erin wheeled around and trudged away. Now what did she do? Why didn't Maria tell her this morning that she was going somewhere? Erin shook off the weird feeling she had about the whole Maria thing. The woman may have simply gone into town. It wasn't like he'd said she was out of the country.

Maybe she'd track down Logan and the others. They had to be around here somewhere.

"And to what do I owe the pleasure of your lovely company?"

Esteban.

A shiver raced up Erin's spine.

Reluctance slowing her, she turned to face him. "I was looking for Maria." She essayed a wide smile.

Esteban closed the distance between them. "Maria is away for the weekend." He set his tumbler of liquor aside on a nearby table. "But I am here. What can *I* do for you?" He moved in so close that Erin battled the urge to run. "I am quite certain you will approve of my readiness to please."

Commanding herself not to tremble, she moistened her lips. "No doubt. But I'm sure Logan will be looking for me by now." Why was she coming up with excuses? This was her chance.

But she wasn't ready for that chance. She knew it the moment she stared into those black eyes. There was a good possibility that she would never be ready to be in a room alone with Pablo Esteban.

"Have a drink with me, my dear," he urged. "Logan and the others are away on a very important errand.''

She drummed up a disappointed frown. ''Without me? Why wasn't I told?''

Esteban smiled suggestively. ''There was no need and someone had to stay behind to entertain me.'' He took her arm and folded it over his own. ''Come. Amuse me.''

Erin didn't miss the wary look on Manuel's face as Esteban escorted her up the grand staircase into forbidden territory…his private quarters. And there was no one nearby to come to her rescue.

She was on her own.

The hope of getting the information they needed warred with the concern for her own safety. She had to try. Her freedom depended upon it. And Logan had said that the longer they stayed here the greater the likelihood of a breach in their cover.

Cortez waited outside Esteban's private suite. Esteban gave him an order that Erin didn't quite understand. Something about surveying something or other. Whatever it was, the man who usually shadowed Esteban's every move disappeared, sending a fresh wave of anxiety through her.

Erin postponed the arrival at Esteban's intended destination by insisting on admiring his Monet once more. He rushed through the answers to her questions. Her heart thumped harder with each passing moment. She'd had six days of training. She was undercover. A spy. She had to do this.

Stay calm, she ordered.

Pay attention to the details.

In Esteban's private parlor, he poured her a finger of brandy. Not much of a drinker, but needing the courage, she downed it in one swallow.

"Another?" He gestured to the decanter.

She nodded, unable to speak as the liquor burned its way down her throat. She'd sip this one, she promised herself.

Details, she reminded herself. Bookcases, books, more artwork, a picturesque view and fine furnishings. No computer. Not even a desk. Like the rest of the house, the room was a pleasure to the eyes, but, she hoped this would not all be for nothing.

She glanced back at Esteban just in time to see him sprinkle some sort of powder into her drink. Fear rocketed through her limbs, banded around her chest. Was he going to kill her or just drug her to ensure her cooperation? She shuddered. Neither alternative held any appeal.

Oh, God. What if he planned to interrogate her?

Those long hours in the Mexican prison reeled through her mind like a video on fast forward. She didn't want to go through that again. And they hadn't used drugs…just intimidation.

Esteban picked up the glasses and turned to her. "Let us toast." He offered her the tainted drink.

Smiling and strutting over to him like a high-priced escort for the evening, she adopted her most seductive voice. She had to distract his attention from the drink. "Why don't we get a little more comfortable first?"

Hunger gleamed in his eyes. "Oh, you are an impatient one." He sat the glasses aside and started to jerk at the buttons of his shirt. "But I understand completely." He practically ripped the hand-tailored fabric from his body. "That husband of yours does not pay proper attention to you." He tossed the shirt aside and moved in on her.

She looped her arms around his neck, repressing the instant revulsion at being close to him. "I'd never think of doing this," she cooed innocently, "if I weren't so starved for the touch of a real man."

Esteban made a little growling sound in his throat. "I will show you what a real man can do."

While he nibbled her neck, she reached for the drink he'd intended for himself. "Wait," she murmured. "I'm so thirsty." When he paused, she drained the glass. "Drink up so we can get down to business."

Esteban smiled knowingly then turned up the other glass and emptied it in one swallow. "To fools," he *clinked* his empty glass against hers. "And Logan is definitely a fool."

Erin had no way of knowing what kind of drug was in the drink or how fast it worked. She could only draw out the play in hopes of it taking effect soon. She made a show of unbuttoning her own blouse and allowing it to slip down her arms. She watched his anticipation turn to desperation as the blouse floated to the floor. Thank God he hadn't noticed she'd switched the drinks.

"Let me help you with that," Esteban insisted, his

speech slightly slurred. He reached around her to help unfasten her bra.

"Wait." Erin slapped his hands away. She was a little dizzy herself. The brandy, she reasoned. She was certain she'd picked up the right glass. "The bedroom, my love. We have to do this right."

Visibly tipsy now, he raised a finger and wagged it at her. "Good point." He manacled her wrist with his iron grip and dragged her into the next room.

Despite his manhandling and the fear still pulsing inside her, Erin's gaze landed instantly on the wide mahogany desk. It was an exact replica of the one in his private office, but this one had a state-of-the-art computer system sitting atop it. This was it. She was in.

Before she realized his intent, he threw her onto the bed and crawled on top of her. A fresh surge of fear rose in her as she looked up into his fierce expression. He was a strong man. Unless the drug took full effect soon she would never be able to fight him off. The urge to scream burgeoned in her throat.

His eyes closed and he wilted, his full body weight collapsing on her, pushing the air straight out of her lungs. Erin struggled to roll him off. She swallowed back the sounds of distress that she couldn't completely restrain. This room might be monitored as well; she couldn't risk anyone overhearing.

She crawled off the bed and just stood there for a moment, catching her breath and making sure he wasn't going to wake up. She pressed her hand to her stomach and closed her eyes for a moment. She thanked God again that the switch had worked.

When her respiration had calmed and he still hadn't moved, she headed for his desk. She touched the mouse and the screen saver disappeared, revealing his electronic desktop. She cringed when she considered that somewhere someone might be listening. She had to keep up the act.

"Oh, yes," she cried, feeling like a fool, but not willing to risk being one. "That's the spot!"

Erin didn't dare sit in the leather chair for fear it would make too much noise. Instead she knelt down and quietly, ever so quietly, started searching for a back door to his security system.

Perspiration slickened her skin as she battled the security system Esteban had in place. It wasn't that sophisticated, just annoying. Every minute or so she would make some high-pitched noise or cry Esteban's name. Whoever was listening was probably convinced by now that Esteban was a god in the sack.

A new screen flashed on the monitor.

She was in!

The file names appeared on the screen like magic. Erin grinned. She was good! The best, she added with well-deserved pride. No one knew cyber security better than her. Usually though, she was building it, not breaching it.

Her grin melted into a frown when she reviewed file after file and found nothing even remotely resembling delivery dates or names or anything else Logan had told her to look for. It was a lot of nothing. Just in case, she took a disk from Esteban's desk and downloaded a copy of everything. There really wasn't that much. And unless Lucas's people saw something she didn't, it was a bust.

Esteban groaned.

Erin quickly logged out and shoved the disk into her back pocket. She rushed to the bed and considered her options. She glanced at the clock and realized more than an hour had passed. Plenty long enough for a date rape. She now had a pretty good idea what the powder had been.

Hating the idea, but knowing it was the only way to retain her cover, she jerked off her clothes and then finished undressing Esteban. She quickly crawled into bed with him and squeezed her eyes shut. Her skin crawled with revulsion. She prayed that this would work without compromising her further. It was bad enough he was going to see her naked.

Slowly, he roused. She snuggled nearer to him. Nausea roiled in her stomach. More than once she wondered if her freedom was worth this humility…this risk.

He nuzzled her neck. "I must have fallen asleep," he murmured thickly.

She stretched as if just waking herself. "Me, too."

He drew back and looked into her face. A frown of confusion lined his brow. "I—"

"Was magnificent," she finished for him, then traced his jaw with her finger. "I hope you enjoyed…" She shrugged self-consciously.

His confusion seemed to deepen for a moment. Erin

held her breath. She was at his mercy...completely. He could scream for Cortez, who probably wasn't far away. She could die, like this in his bed. She shuddered inwardly. Please, please let him believe her.

He smiled finally. "You were everything I knew you would be." He smoothed a hand down her rib cage. Ice formed in her middle. "In fact, I think we should have an encore."

She wriggled away from him. "I should go. Logan might be back and—"

Esteban pulled her to him. "I want you to stay."

She looked him straight in the eye and hoped like hell this would work. "He can't find out. He'll kill you if he finds out."

Esteban smirked. "You mean he'll try."

"Yes," she said solemnly. "He will."

That realization seemed to finally sink in. "Logan is a good man. I want him on my team." Esteban's gaze roved her nude body. She steeled herself against a shudder. "As much as I want you again, I will not risk his wrath. We shall keep this discreet."

She nodded, too weak with relief to speak.

She struggled into her clothes, keeping her back away from Esteban for fear he might notice the disk in her pocket. When she pulled on her blouse, she left it hanging loose from her jeans so it would cover her pockets. She slipped on her shoes, not bothering to tie them.

Esteban pulled on his trousers and moved to the parlor to make himself another drink.

He snagged her arm when she would have rushed

past him. "You will come to me again soon, I will see to it."

"Yes."

He released her. "Discretion," he reminded.

She nodded and hurried from the room. Cortez smirked at her as she flew past him. She felt queasy, dirty. Taking the stairs two at a time, she almost fell in her haste. Her heart threatened to burst from her chest. She had to get out of here. Realization of what she had done had only now penetrated the heady rush of success...however short-lived.

"Halt!"

She skidded to a stop not five feet from the door. Her heart stuttered in her chest. She swore softly. So close. Had Manuel noticed the disk in her pocket? Had Esteban realized what she'd done?

Manuel approached her. Walked all the way around her, scrutinizing her, while her fear soared to a new level.

He finally leaned in close and whispered. "You are playing with fire, *senorita*. Make no mistake."

Erin nodded, her limbs trembling so badly that she could hardly stand at this point.

"Go," he muttered.

Erin forced herself to walk once she'd gotten outside. The last thing she wanted to do was attract attention. By the time she reached their quarters, tears were streaming down her face. She closed and locked the door, then sagged against it.

"Where the hell have you been?"

She looked up.

Logan.

Chapter Ten

Logan stared at the disk Erin held in one shaky hand.

Esteban's files.

There was only one way she'd gotten into his private files.

"I asked," he repeated, the anger in his voice was, unfortunately, not forced, "where the hell have you been?"

She trembled, but understood where he was going with his demand. He saw the comprehension in her eyes. The fear residing there as well tied his gut in knots.

"Nowhere special," she said, her voice quaking. "Just out."

"I don't believe you." Logan considered where was the best hiding place for the disk until he could get it to Ferrelli. "You're lying," he accused harshly.

"I'm telling the truth," she argued. She moved toward the telephone table where her purse sat and opened the drawer. "I don't care if you believe me or not."

He glanced at the Bible inside the drawer and nodded. "You'd better care," he growled as she placed the disk inside the black, leather bound Bible. "Don't make me get rough with you, Baby." He didn't take the time to consider why a man like Esteban would keep a Bible around. Maybe it was one of Maria's touches.

"Don't threaten me." Her voice warbled.

Logan turned back to Erin, she looked ready to crumple. She trembled. Her complexion was deathly pale. Whatever had happened, she was badly shaken. The urge to kill Esteban detonated inside him. Logan pulled her to him. She sagged in his hold, sobbed softly against his shirt.

"Did he hurt you?" he murmured against her ear, his rage barely restrained. "Tell me if he hurt you."

She shook her head, fresh tears rolling down her cheeks. "No," she whimpered.

"I'm sorry, Baby, I didn't mean to make you cry," he said more for her benefit than for the hidden microphones.

He scooped her up and went to the sofa. He sat down, cradling her protectively in his arms. "Shhh. It's okay. I'm not angry anymore."

And it was true. His anger had taken a back seat to his desire to comfort her. To his need to make this right. He couldn't bear to see her like this…couldn't bear the idea that Esteban might have touched her in any way. He should never have agreed to that run into Medellín this morning. The entire business had been a waste of time. He, better than anyone, knew Esteban didn't waste time. He'd wanted Logan out of the way.

Her arms were around his neck, her cheek soft against his shoulder. "It was a bust," she whispered.

Frowning he leaned closer. "The files are nothing," she murmured so softly he barely heard her.

His arms tightened around her. If that was true…right now he just didn't care. He inclined his head closer to hers. "Did he touch you?" There was no way to keep the ferocity out of his voice or the battle-ready tension out of his body.

She rose up, looked directly into his eyes and shook her head.

Thank God. Logan exhaled a shaky breath. If he'd ever been more relieved to hear anything, he had no recall of the event. If Esteban had touched her that way, Logan wasn't sure he could have handled it. Not for a second had he fully realized that truth until that moment.

He didn't want anyone else touching Erin like that. Only him.

But even he didn't deserve her and he certainly wasn't worthy of her trust. He touched her cheek, slid one finger along the line of her jaw. She trembled. His gut clenched. He'd allowed this to happen to her. He could have said no to Lucas and Casey, but she'd had no choice.

When she learned the whole truth, she would never forgive him.

LOGAN SPENT Saturday evening and all day Sunday avoiding Esteban. He just wasn't sure he could keep his cool considering he'd spent the night consoling

Erin. He'd held her, his body aching to do far more, but knowing that comfort was what she needed most.

Making love to her was out of the question. He was holding back information from her that would change their whole relationship. He blew out a self-deprecating breath. This wasn't supposed to be about a relationship. It was about the mission. His job. Nothing else. Erin Bailey was a pawn. One he'd willingly used and he doubted she would forgive him for it when she learned the truth.

He tossed aside the cloth he'd been using to clean his weapon. Too many hours alone with Erin had brought him here, to the ammunition room. He'd needed some space to get his head clear.

Hinges creaked.

Logan jerked his gaze upward, the weapon in his hand leveling on the threat.

Cortez.

"Esteban will see you in his office."

Logan shoved the weapon into the back of his jeans. "Whatever Esteban wants, he gets, right?" he said sarcastically.

Cortez's smug expression was answer enough. Fury twisted inside Logan. He was going to thoroughly enjoy taking down these guys.

ESTEBAN WAITED in his private office. A lit cigar in his hand. "Logan, my friend, would you care for a smoke?" he offered by way of greeting.

"No, thanks." Logan allowed him to see a certain level of unhappiness in his expression.

"Well, then." Esteban eased down on the edge of his desk. "Please, have a seat."

"I'll stand." Logan was pushing the envelope, he knew by the outrage that flashed in Esteban's black eyes, but he ignored it. Reveled in it actually.

Esteban took a long drag from his cigar, then blew out the smoke. "I have been watching you, Logan," he said finally. "You impressed me on your first assignment, but I have become even more aware of your ability to organize and stay focused during this past week."

Logan inclined his head in a careless shrug. "I take my work seriously."

"Indeed." Another long pause for a drag. "I need more men like you. It is not necessary to tell you every little thing to do. You are a 'take charge' fellow. Very rare in this business."

Logan folded his arms over his chest. "Is there somewhere specific you're going with this conversation?"

Esteban smiled. "You are angry with me." He waved his hand in dismissal. "You should not be concerned." His gaze grew more pointed. "I have plans for you, Logan. Very big plans."

Speculation was pointless. Esteban's suggestion could range from a promotion to a one-way ticket six feet under. "That's good to hear," he relented. He'd pressed his luck with the attitude far enough.

Esteban tapped out his cigar and left it in the large crystal ashtray. "Tonight I will introduce you to many important men who work for me in other capacities."

Drug lords, Logan filled in the blanks.

"On Monday you will take lead on a very important assignment for me. If you handle it properly, you will discover just how generous I can be." He stood and leveled a warning gaze on Logan. "If, however, you fail me, then you will learn how exacting I am in carrying out punishment."

Logan relaxed his stance a bit. "Fair enough."

Esteban offered his hand. "Let us seal our deal then."

Logan took the offered hand, fully aware of the great significance the gesture carried. Esteban trusted him.

Nothing could stop Logan now.

He was in all the way.

ERIN SLIPPED ON the black high-heeled shoes Logan had bought her to go with the little black dress. "Little" being the operative word here. The dress clung to her like a second skin and left absolutely nothing to the imagination. She'd actually selected this particular one, but only after she'd seen the look on his face when she tried it on.

She peered at her reflection in the mirror as she twisted her hair up into a little bun that didn't look quite elegant, but would do. The bruise was practically gone now. A little of her recently purchased concealer had taken care of the lingering discoloration. She thought a moment of how the guy who'd left that mark on her had warned her about playing with fire. Could it be that he actually felt he owed her one? She wasn't going to put any stock in that idea.

Erin stepped back and studied her reflection. Good enough, she decided, for rubbing shoulders with Colombia's most elite pond scum.

A long, low whistle sent her whirling toward the door. Logan was openly admiring her. "I'm not sure it'll be safe to let you go looking like that."

Erin blushed. How could he look at her like that and act so impressed when he'd already seen all there was to see? The way he'd held her last night and whispered consoling words into her ear made her feel weak and giddy all over again. He'd understood how dirty she'd felt. She'd known he understood fully when he drew her a hot bath and ushered her into it. She wondered how many times in his business he'd had to do things he'd despised. Too many probably.

"You don't look so bad yourself, Lover," she teased, but it was true. He looked fantastic in that suit. The slacks and jacket were black, the shirt white and open at the throat. He looked amazing. And as sexy as hell.

Logan offered his arm. "Shall we go?"

Erin curled her arm through his and breathed deeply of his tantalizing masculine scent. His aftershave was so subtle, just a hint of something spicy. Even when she hadn't seen him all day, she could close her eyes and conjure up that sexy, unique scent.

With the full moon spilling its golden glow over their path, an epiphany dawned on her as they strode through the cool night air toward the main house. She trusted Logan completely. After last night, she'd even be willing to trust him with her heart. She smiled sadly when she confessed to herself what that tangle of emotions meant.

She'd fallen for the guy.

Gloom enveloped her on the heels of that thought. It was the worst thing that could have happened and yet she wouldn't have traded knowing him this way for anything. But the fact remained that there was absolutely no future in this relationship. There was only here and now…and even that was make-believe.

The party was well under way when they arrived. Until tonight, Erin had only been as far as the briefing room downstairs. Upstairs, of course, was another story. One she didn't intend to dwell upon. But at the end of the immense entry hall and well beyond the dining room and kitchen, there was a huge room for entertaining that spanned the entire length of the house. Several French doors opened onto the elegant terrace.

Erin recognized the tables outside as Sheila's favorite lounging space. Speaking of the wicked witch, Erin scanned the crowd until she located her. Dressed in a royal blue dress that was even shorter and tighter than Erin's, Sheila was surrounded by doting admirers.

Logan had immediately been dragged by Esteban into a large group of older men. The local drug lords, she imagined. Logan had told her during their late-afternoon run all that Esteban had guaranteed him. It was the first time she and Logan had run together since their arrival. She was afraid to put too much stock in his sudden desire to spend extra time with her. It was probably just the only situation he considered safe enough in which to pass along the information.

This new offer from Esteban was good, Logan had explained. This way, if they gleaned nothing from the disk, Logan would be in a position to uncover the needed information eventually. Erin just wasn't sure how long she could keep up the front. If Esteban approached her again...

She couldn't handle it. She'd told Logan as much. He'd understood and had agreed to intervene. That had surprised her. The idea that he would risk blowing his cover for her shook her to the core. She reached for a glass of champagne as a waiter passed. Maybe Logan felt something more for her.

Get real, Erin, she chastised. He's probably done this dozens of times before. It was his job to protect her, he'd told her that from the beginning. The subtle shift she thought she'd noticed in him was probably just wishful thinking.

Just when Erin had started to wonder about Maria being away and missing all the hoopla, the woman appeared. She looked absolutely royal in a white dress that was both demure and sensual. Each of Esteban's associates turned to look when she walked into the room. Erin watched Esteban's reaction to the attention his sister received and was not surprised to find she'd been right. He didn't like it one little bit. He glowered at the group of men surrounding him, then said something that quickly garnered their wayward attention.

Erin took a quick sip of her champagne, set the

stemmed glass aside and wove through the crowd to reach Maria. Erin waited until the woman had finished greeting those closest to her before saying hello.

"Maria, I'm so glad you're back," Erin said in all honesty. "I was afraid you'd miss the party."

Maria looked confused for a moment, but quickly recovered. "I never miss my brother's parties. It is the one occasion when there is much happiness."

Erin couldn't help a twinge of sympathy for the woman. She apparently lived under Esteban's iron fist and had no outside life other than her flowers.

"Was your trip successful? Did you bring back any new varieties?"

Maria patted her arm affectionately. "I did. But I'm afraid you wouldn't recognize their names. It will be many weeks before their true beauty is revealed."

"I look forward to seeing them," Erin enthused. "Your garden is the most beautiful part of the estate."

Maria smiled, a blush staining her cheeks. She was the most humble person Erin had ever met. She couldn't imagine how the woman retained such humility in this environment. The thought occurred to Erin that perhaps Maria was not fully aware of the true nature of Esteban's business dealings.

Then again, she had been present when Esteban suggested Erin shoot that guard. But that might be an everyday part of the macho culture in Colombia. Perhaps that was why Maria didn't buck her subservient lifestyle. Erin thought of the street children and the mothers left to bear the burden of raising them alone.

Maybe Maria considered her brother's harsh ways the lesser of the evils.

"Let us mingle," Maria suggested, taking Erin's arm. "My brother has many friends as you can see."

Did that mean they weren't Maria's friends as well? Erin tried not to analyze everything the woman said, but it was difficult not to. Erin couldn't understand a seemingly intelligent woman's willingness to hold such a lowly position. Despite the hurt her ex-fiancé had wielded, Erin couldn't imagine giving up the equal rights she enjoyed as a woman in the United States. Surely Maria had traveled there and had seen what she was missing.

"Where did you go to find your new flowers?" Erin asked before she thought the question completely through. She almost cringed in hindsight. The woman would think she was nosy. Or worse, that she was a spy trying to interrogate her. "I'm sorry, I didn't mean to pry," she added quickly.

Maria smiled again. "Don't be silly. It is not a secret that I travel frequently. Sometimes even to Europe." She sighed wistfully. "It is the only time I feel truly complete. I enjoy my little hobby so very much."

The features of her face tightened, as if she'd said more than she intended. "What a poor hostess I am," she said quickly. "We should talk about you, not someone so boring as myself."

Erin tensed. "Oh, there really isn't much to tell."

Maria waved over a waiter. "Don't be modest. I wish to know about your life." She took a fluted glass from the silver tray the waiter offered. *"Gracias."* The waiter nodded and moved away.

"You are educated?" Maria prodded, taking a sip of the fine champagne.

A brittle smile in place, Erin struggled to remember the backstory for her cover. What college was in Austin? Damn. She had no idea. "I started at a local community college," she winged it. "But I got engaged and dropped out."

"Ah." Maria nodded. "You met Logan."

She and Logan were supposed to have been together for three years. She was how old? "Actually," she hedged. "There was another guy before him." She sipped her bubbly and tried not to act as nervous as she suddenly felt. Somehow it just felt wrong lying to someone as nice as Maria. "He was a total jerk and..." She exhaled a stress-filled breath. "Well, he broke my heart." She blinked back the emotion that welled in her eyes. Damn. She should be over that by now. It wasn't Jeff so much anymore as it was her own stupidity that got to her. How could she have been so blind?

Maria shook her head slowly. "Men. They can be such animals." She glanced at her brother. "Pigs."

Erin was surprised by the woman's vehemence. "Some guys are definite pigs," she agreed.

"Most are," Maria countered firmly. "Watch yourself, Sara."

Erin was always brought up short by the name, she heard it so rarely.

"You cannot trust any of them," Maria went on.

"Perhaps your Logan is different." She studied Logan then. "It is hard to know."

"He's special," Erin heard herself say. She frowned, but admitted that it was true. "He takes good care of me."

Maria's gaze locked with hers. "Still, you must be careful. No man is above using a woman for his own best interests."

Erin promised, "I will."

Maria turned and greeted the next person who approached, her entire persona changing to dutiful sister...elegant lady. What terrible things had Esteban or his friends done to her? Erin suddenly wanted to smuggle Maria away. To insist that Logan's people hide her in the witness protection program or whatever they called it. The woman was a prisoner. Esteban probably sent two armed guards with her everywhere she went just to make sure she didn't speak to anyone she shouldn't.

How sad for her. Erin wondered then what would become of Maria when Logan brought down her brother. Would she be penniless and living on the streets? Erin ached at the thought. Somehow she had to make sure that didn't happen.

The idea of warning Maria so that she could get away before it was too late flitted through Erin's mind. She'd have to give that some thought. Whatever she did to help the woman she'd have to make sure it didn't endanger Logan's life. After all Esteban was Maria's brother. Maria had been raised in a completely different culture from Erin. She might not see this the way Erin did when it came to her brother's fate.

There was time for Erin to decide. Time to dig more deeply into the situation to see if the woman really did need saving or even if she wanted to be saved. The vehemence in her voice when she spoke of men echoed in Erin's ears. She had a very strong feeling that there might not be that much love lost between Maria and her brother.

LOGAN WATCHED Erin from across the room all night. She looked terrific. Every move she made took his breath. Any time a member of the male species came close to her, his blood boiled with a raging possessiveness. He wanted her for himself.

Esteban's constant attention made him want to say to hell with the mission, but that was crazy. This thing between him and Erin was just a fluke…a passing fancy. It would be over soon and another mission would take its place. Still, Logan had never had this much trouble staying focused.

He shouldn't now.

He was glad Esteban's sister had spent the better part of the evening glued to Erin's side. Even when Esteban had gotten a little too friendly, Maria had stepped in and ushered Erin in another direction. Logan liked the woman more and more.

Maybe she was aware of her brother's lasciviousness and hoped to save Erin from him. Whatever the case, Logan was extremely grateful.

As soon as he could make the rounds to the necessary people, he and Erin were out of here.

Just before Logan reached Erin, Sheila Watters snagged her arm and pulled her to one side. Logan moved closer to hear what the woman had to say. He'd noticed her animosity toward Erin.

"Listen, you little bitch," Sheila hissed. "This is your last warning. If you don't stay away from Esteban, I'm going to kill you myself."

Erin jerked free of her hold. "I don't know what you're talking about."

"Right," the woman accused. "You'd better be careful or I'll get you and your husband, too. I've already been telling Larry how your man flirts with me. If I push the issue, he'll take Logan out."

So that's why Larry had been giving him the evil eye lately. Logan had wondered if the man simply didn't like Esteban's favor being cast in Logan's direction. Now he knew.

Logan moved in next to Erin and wrapped her arm around his. "Good night, Sheila," he said to the startled woman. "Maybe if Larry finds out how you chase after Esteban, he'll pay more attention to you."

Her eyes rounded and then narrowed and shifted to Erin. "Just remember what I said." She spun on her heel and strode away.

Erin stayed close to Logan's side on the way to their quarters. He couldn't be sure if what Sheila said had gotten to her or if it was Esteban's constant pawing. He sighed. Damn, he wanted so badly to protect her from all this, except he kept failing miserably.

Inside, Erin hurried to the bedroom, her hands going immediately to the zipper of her dress. He stalled halfway across the front room, unable to move as he watched the dress slide down her bare skin and puddle on the floor. A thong bared her heart-shaped rear and there was no bra. Just lots and lots of creamy smooth skin and dangerous curves. She released her hair and combed her fingers through it. His mouth parched. Every muscle in his body hardened.

God, how he wanted her. He could still remember how she tasted, how smooth her skin felt, how intensely she'd responded to his touch. Something deep inside him shifted, broke free.

She shimmied into a T-shirt and the show was over. But Logan would never be the same again.

Chapter Eleven

Esteban held his briefing at dawn.

Larry Watters was not happy when Logan was assigned lead, but he knew better than to rock the boat. Whatever Esteban wanted, Esteban got.

The aircraft that took the four of them, the Watterses, Logan and Erin, was very similar to the one Mission Recovery used. Executive size, Learjet. Luxurious enough and fast enough. Every illegal arms dealer/drug lord's dream ride. Near Canoga Park, just outside Los Angeles, the aircraft touched down at an airstrip privately owned by a local corporation who laundered money for Esteban.

A black, stretch limousine waited.

Once they deplaned, each carrying a steel briefcase, Logan checked his watch. "We'll be back in two hours. Be fueled and ready to go," he instructed Hector Caldarone who served as their pilot.

The briefcases, which contained a rather large quantity of Esteban's powdered merchandise, were quickly stored in the limo's trunk before the group climbed into the luxurious automobile.

Inside, Logan leaned forward and asked the driver, "You've got the address?"

"Yes, sir. ETA is seventeen minutes."

Logan nodded. "Perfect."

No one spoke as the limo eased through one crowded street after the other, coming ever nearer to their destination. This would be Logan's only chance to get the disk containing Esteban's computer files to Lucas. But Larry watched Logan like a hawk, just hoping to see a wrong move. Still, determining whether the information they needed was on that disk or not was vital. There was always the possibility it was coded. Erin had no way of knowing for certain. Instinct nudged Logan, warning him that she was most likely right on the money, but they had to be certain.

Noticing an upcoming fast-food restaurant, Logan tapped on the privacy glass. When it slid down, he said, "How about going through that drive-thru coming up on the right. I'm starved. How about you, Baby?"

Erin smiled. "Famished."

"We can eat later," Larry argued. "We don't want to be late for our meet."

"Are we going to be late if we take this little detour?" Logan asked the driver.

"No, sir."

"Good."

Larry and Sheila fumed as Logan instructed the driver to order a couple of burgers and colas. Adding insult to injury, he and Erin moaned with pleasure as they ate. Though Logan had to admit that some of his pleasure was derived from looking at Erin's long, bare legs displayed so pleasingly by that short denim skirt she wore. The shopping trip had paid off in more ways than one.

At Larry's continued glower, Logan couldn't help but smile. There was something the guy would have to learn about his chosen profession.

Nothing stayed the same in this business. Most of the players didn't live long enough to notice.

When they reached the rendezvous point, Logan emerged first, scanning warily to see that all was clear. He tossed the fast-food bag, which now contained the disk, on the ground near the side of the building.

The driver had parked between two long warehouses. The place looked exactly as Esteban had described it—quiet and deserted. If Esteban's intelligence was correct, both warehouses were currently unoccupied and for lease. So far, Logan hadn't really been able to tell who was feeding Esteban his information. Whoever it was, he was good.

While Larry and the ladies unloaded the goods from the trunk, Logan had a talk with the driver.

"Step out of the car," he ordered.

The guy looked hesitant.

"Now." Logan fixed him with a look that dared him to decline.

The driver clambered from behind the wheel, fear making him clumsy. "If something's wrong, sir—"

"Nothing is wrong. I need your wallet."

Confusion claimed the driver's face.

Logan nodded and held out his hand. The wallet

quickly appeared in his palm. He opened it and studied the driver's license. "Danny Marsh." He glanced at the driver. "You still live at 103 Oakley Lane?"

Marsh nodded, his eyes like saucers.

Logan flipped through the pictures until he found a family photo of Danny, a woman and two kids. "This your wife and kids?"

He nodded again.

"A beautiful family." Logan returned his wallet. "Listen to me, Danny. We've got some very important business to take care of. Sometimes things don't go the way we plan and we get a little rowdy."

"Don't worry, sir. I never hear or see anything." He shook his head. "Never."

"That's good." Logan leaned closer. "But I don't want to come back out here and find this alley empty, you understand what I'm saying?"

Danny nodded vigorously.

"Good. So, no matter what you hear or see, you're staying put, right?"

Another enthusiastic nod.

Logan leveled a hard gaze on him. "Just remember, Danny, I know where you live. Don't leave me hanging."

"No, sir." He swiped his sweating brow. "Wouldn't think of it, sir."

"That's my man." Logan slapped him on the back and joined the others at the rear of the vehicle.

"You expecting trouble?" Larry demanded.

"I always cover all the bases, buddy," Logan told him as he took the briefcase Erin carried. "Always."

As Esteban predicted, the warehouse they entered was empty save for one long table. The briefcases were placed side by side on the table, then unlocked and opened. Their contact would arrive any minute now and the deal would go down.

"Baby, you and Sheila cover that entrance," Logan ordered. "Larry and I will take care of things on this end."

The building was one long structure, with overhead doors, as well as walk-thrus on each end.

When Erin and Sheila were in position, Logan moved back to the table where Larry waited.

"I want you to know I don't like this," Larry told him flatly.

Big surprise. "I can see that." Logan assessed the other man's expression. "But you'll have to live with it."

Tension thickened between them for several seconds before Larry responded. "I guess I will. At least until you screw up and Esteban realizes his mistake."

Logan dipped his head in acknowledgment of the challenge. "Don't hold your breath."

Erin watched the tense exchange between Watters and Logan. She knew for certain that Sheila couldn't be trusted and doubted if Larry could. She was relatively certain that's why Logan had stationed her at his back, to cover him.

The grating sound of a heavy overhead door being opened drew Erin's gaze to the far end of the warehouse. The large drive-through door rolled upward revealing the front end of another black limo like the one they'd arrived in.

"'Bout time," Sheila muttered.

"You know these guys?"

She glared at Erin as if she were too ignorant to comprehend a simple yes or no. "I didn't fall off the turnip truck yesterday. Yeah, I know 'em. Unlike you, we've been working this territory for some time now."

Erin nodded. "So what'd you do before this? Cosmetology?" Sheila's hair was a different shade of red today. In the last week, she'd changed the color three times.

She sneered. "You're funny. I knew a girl once who was funny like you." She withdrew her weapon and caressed her cheek with it. "I had to kill her. She got on my nerves something awful."

The limo drove straight to where Logan and Watters stood. When it stopped, three men emerged. All wearing dark business suits and dark glasses. Erin kept forgetting hers. Logan and the Watterses never left home without their designer shades. Erin was really behind the curve. A whole week on the job and she still couldn't remember to properly accessorize.

The three men joined Logan at the table where the merchandise awaited their perusal. The packaging was inspected and finally one was selected for purity testing. Just like in the movies, Erin thought. Only she was here watching...participating.

She shivered. How many more times would they have to do this before it was over? She thought about how she'd lain in bed next to Logan last night. Sleep had been slow in coming. And every second of every minute she'd wanted him. Yearned for him. He'd wanted her, too. She'd sensed it. But he held back. Didn't want to cross the line except when necessary to facilitate the mission.

Erin couldn't see any way out of this without serious damage to her already battered heart. But maybe Logan was doing the right thing by not allowing things between them to get more complicated. Although, as far as she was concerned, they were already pretty complicated.

Just the sound of Logan's voice among the other men's made her long to touch him. The deep resonance of it tugged at her senses. Made her want to know him outside this setting, these boundaries.

But that wouldn't happen because he was too dedicated to duty. He wasn't the marrying kind. He wasn't even the falling in love kind.

Erin sighed. Life really did suck sometimes. Just when she thought it couldn't get any worse, something else kicked her in the teeth.

One of the rear passenger doors on the limo opened and a young Latino got out. Unlike the others, he wasn't wearing a suit, just dark slacks and a white shirt. Erin's tension ratcheted up a notch. He sniffed and wiped his nose as if he'd just inhaled a hit of cocaine.

Erin rolled her eyes. God, she hated these people.

Logan had assured her that the drugs they carried would be confiscated before they got a block from this warehouse. Erin did not want to be responsible for even one ounce of cocaine hitting the streets.

The man who'd just gotten out of the limo started toward the others, but hesitated to take a second look in her direction. His gaze settled squarely on Erin. Just what she needed, she mused wryly. Some dopehead coming over to flirt with her.

As the tall, thin man neared, recognition flared in his eyes. Erin suppressed the very nearly overwhelming urge to run like hell. He raised his arm, aiming a long finger accusingly at her.

"You're *dead,*" he murmured. "I killed you."

Erin stiffened. What was he talking about?

"Who is this jerk?" Sheila demanded.

He shook his head. "You're dead!" he shouted, repeatedly stabbing his finger at Erin. "I killed you!"

Before Erin could react he had drawn his weapon and stuck it in her face. "I don't care how many times I have to kill you—"

The rest of his tirade ended with the small round hole that appeared in the center of his forehead. He fell forward, right into Erin's arms. She screamed. Her heart surged into her throat.

All hell broke loose. Weapons fired. Erin dropped to the concrete floor using the dead guy for cover. The sound of weapons discharging echoed in the building. Curses and heated instructions were shouted. She shuddered and huddled more deeply behind the body. Fear ravaged her. Paralyzed her. She wanted to check on Logan, but didn't dare move. What was she supposed to do? Her brief training had not prepared her for this.

But she couldn't just stay here and do nothing. She had to know…to help. She had to do something.

Only two men were standing when Erin peered up from her makeshift hiding place, Logan and a newcomer all dressed in black, ski mask included.

Sheila screamed. She dropped her weapon and rushed to her husband, falling to her knees beside his motionless body.

Erin struggled up, her weapon clenched in her fingers. She stumbled away from the body at her feet.

Logan moved toward her. The other man removed his mask and Erin recognized him immediatcly as the man who'd flirted with her in Medellín on Saturday. The one who'd followed them to the restaurant. Logan had called him their guardian angel. He didn't look much like an angel then and damn sure didn't now.

"Are you all right?" Logan surveyed her for damage, his gaze concerned, fearful even.

"I'm okay." She waved him away. "You'd better check on Sheila."

An ear-piercing shriek cut through the air. Sheila grabbed her husband's weapon and took a bead on Logan.

"You did this!" she screamed.

The explosion of the weapon firing came in slow motion for Erin. She tried to push Logan out of the way. The bullet glanced off the floor a few feet away. Then there was silence.

Sheila collapsed atop her husband's body. Ferrelli

had taken her out. Erin hadn't even heard his shot. A closer look at his weapon explained the absence of sound, he used a sound suppresser. Logan had told her about those.

"The disk is in a fast-food bag on the ground near the limo." Logan shoved his weapon into his waistband. "I have no additional intel."

Ferrelli surveyed the collateral damage including the driver for the second limo slumped near the driver's side door. "I'll call Housekeeping."

"Thanks."

Logan's arm went around Erin's trembling shoulders. "We have to get back. We'll take the drugs and the money. Maybe that'll appease Esteban when he finds out things went to hell again."

Erin looked back at the dead man who'd claimed he'd already killed her once. "Who was that guy?"

"His name's Sanchez." Logan stared at the man with pure hatred. "He's the weasel who killed Jess."

No wonder he looked as if he'd seen a ghost. Erin shuddered. He'd thought she was the real Jess, Logan's former partner.

"Thank you," she remembered to say to Ferrelli, "for saving my life."

Ferrelli smiled. When he did, his gray eyes danced. Erin was sure she'd never seen a man with more compelling eyes. She hugged her arms around Logan. Well, except for Logan's.

"I'm glad I could take him down for you and for Jess," Ferrelli said, then gifted Erin with a flirtatious wink. "Anything else I can do before you two roll?"

"Just tell Lucas to find something on that disk, things are getting too hot around here," Logan answered.

"Will do."

Erin was too shaken to protest, but she already knew they wouldn't find anything. Wherever Esteban kept his private working files, it wasn't on his PC.

As Logan had ordered, the limo driver waited right where he'd left him.

Ferrelli and Logan loaded the money and drugs into the trunk. Ferrelli snatched up the burger bag and waved a little salute of farewell before disappearing into the shadows farther down the alley.

Erin slid into the limo, her legs too weak from receding adrenaline to hold her upright any longer. She trembled violently as her gaze met Danny's equally fearful one in the rearview mirror.

"Don't worry," she said, her voice weary. "We're the good guys."

He exhaled a mighty breath, going for a chuckle but not quite hitting the mark.

Logan settled into the seat next to Erin and closed his door. "Let's go."

The limo rolled into forward motion. Erin closed her eyes and dropped her head against the seat. How would they ever explain this to Esteban?

They were dead.

"Don't worry," Logan said softly. "It'll be all right."

She opened her eyes and looked at him. Really looked at him. She wondered how he could be so calm after all that had happened. How could he simply go back and face Esteban with this news and not sweat the repercussions?

She shook her head. "No it won't. It won't ever be all right again."

Concern crept into his handsome features. "I'll make it right." One fingertip traced a path down her cheek. She shivered in reaction. "You have my word on that."

Erin stared deeply into Logan's dark, dark eyes and saw her reflection there. Saw a woman in love with a man she would never have…couldn't possibly dream of having. And time was slipping away. In just a few hours they might both be dead. There was no more time to waste.

"I'm afraid your word isn't going to be enough." She pulled his face down to hers and kissed him hard on the mouth.

He kissed her back, not quite with abandon, but with a slow building, restrained passion she could feel simmering just beneath the surface.

She quickly released the buttons of his shirt and slid her hands over the magnificent terrain of his chest. She wanted to touch all of him…to feel the warmth of his skin against hers, flesh to flesh.

"Whoa," he murmured against her lips. He reached for her roaming hands. "We need to slow this down."

"No." She pulled his unbuttoned shirt from the waistband of his jeans. "No more waiting…no more pretending."

She wrapped her arms around his neck and pulled

his mouth back to hers. She knew the instant he made up his mind. The passion erupted to the surface, unbridled hunger made him bolder, more aggressive. He pushed her down onto the soft leather seat, kissing her lips, her chin, her throat.

He reached up, pounded on the glass with the flat of his palm.

"Yes, sir?"

Logan broke free from the kiss just long enough to say, "We'll need a little more privacy and a lot more than seventeen minutes."

"Whatever you say, sir."

Erin would swear she heard a smile in the driver's voice. The privacy shield came up between the passenger compartment and the driver's seat. And for the first time in more than a week, they were completely alone with no one listening or watching, only the needing and wanting throbbing in the silence.

Logan urged her to a sitting position as his fingers caught in the hem of her blouse. He pulled it over her head and tossed it aside. For one long moment he simply stared at her satin-and-lace encased breasts. He moistened his lips, the move sending an electrical current straight to the juncture of her thighs. Moisture pooled there, anticipating his touch.

The limo ride was as smooth as glass. Just like Logan's long-fingered hands when he lifted her breasts from their confines, first one, then the other. He tucked the satin cups beneath her breasts, making them tilt upward and outward for his attention. Kneeling before her, he leaned forward and made a wide circle around one breast with his tongue. Erin moaned softly and braced her hands against the seat.

He made achingly slow circles, each time around the circle grew smaller, his tongue eased nearer to her swollen nipple. Then he took it into his hot, steamy mouth. Sucked hard. Her hips lifted from the seat. She bit back a scream.

He did the same with the other nipple, taking his sweet time, drawing out the pleasure. Making her crazy with need. Her hips moved restlessly, instinctively mimicking an age-old rhythm that played deep in her soul. His fingers tightened around her rib cage as he pressed his mouth more fully over her left breast.

She couldn't wait any longer. She had to touch him. Her fingers buried in his thick hair. She urged his hungry mouth to take more of her. His hands traveled down to her thighs and she begged him to touch her there, not with words, but with her body's desperate language.

Those magical hands slid up her thighs, beneath her skirt. His fingers curled in her panties and dragged the skimpy things down and off her legs.

She was wet. So wet. The feel of that one finger as it slipped inside her, had her arching against his hand. She wanted more of him inside her. Now!

"Enough." She pushed him away from her tingling breast and fumbled with the closure of his jeans. She whimpered when she couldn't open them quickly enough. He helped, easing down the zipper. His erection sprang free, pleasantly surprising her. She'd forgotten he didn't wear underwear. She was so glad he didn't. She touched him. Encircled that silken part of him. He groaned. Another wave of urgency flooded her. Now. She wanted *that* part of him now.

She shoved his pants beneath his hips and ushered him onto the seat. She straddled him. He caught her waist in both hands and prevented her desperate downward plunge.

"Wait," he breathed.

She shook her head. "No more waiting." She pressed herself against his straining tip. He made an animal sound in his throat. "Now," she moaned.

He released a ragged breath. "There are things…" He growled when she brushed her wet feminine channel along his tip. "…things you need to know."

She encircled him with cool steady fingers and guided him to her entrance, pressing down as hard as she could, fighting his hold. "Later." She cried out as she took an inch of him inside her.

His restraining hold weakened. Another inch eased inside. She couldn't utter a sound…she could scarcely breathe. She was unbelievably tight. It had been so, so long. Or maybe it was just Logan…

She pressed down another inch, relishing the exquisite feeling of penetration…of stretching. His fingers bit into the flesh of her waist. He was shaking now with the effort of restraint. Release was already building inside her. Tightening her muscles… drenching them both in her liquid heat.

She put her hands on his shoulders and looked straight into his eyes. "I know all I need to."

Something changed in that dark, dark gaze. A clarity that chased away the doubts. A need that over-whelmed all else. His features a study in desire and desperation, he allowed her downward progress, inch after hot, hard inch, until he fully sheathed his thick length inside her...until her throbbing bud nestled firmly against his male flesh.

Climax was instantaneous.

Never breaking the seal of intense joining, he lowered her to the seat, putting himself in the dominant position. He drew back, thrust hard into her. Repeated the delicious action. Again. Faster. Harder. His muscles tense...his gaze primal, piercing, looking right into her soul as he climbed upward, upward toward his own pinnacle. She climaxed again, this time the full body kind of release that went on and on.

He came hard...roaring with it. His muscles corded to the point of snapping, his rigid length pulsing, plunging once, twice more.

He held his weight off her, his arms trembling with the weakness of his recent release. He kissed her again, slowly, softly, making her whimper with the sweetness of it. They'd forgotten all about kissing in those last desperate minutes. They could only stare into each other's eyes. But now, the kiss went on and on, drawing on her heartstrings with the incredible tenderness of it.

He drew away just far enough to look into her eyes, his expression tormented. "We have to talk."

Chapter Twelve

"We don't have much time."

Erin leaned against the limo watching Logan stalk back and forth in front of her. The driver had taken them to an out-of-the-way place not far from the airfield.

We have to talk. Logan had said those words to her while he was still deep inside her and he hadn't spoken another word to her until now. Dread pooled in her stomach. She was suddenly certain that she didn't want to hear whatever it was he had to tell her.

"So tell me already," she said pushing away from the shiny black vehicle.

Logan stared at the ground for a second that dragged into five. "It's my fault you're in this."

The statement startled her so that she laughed. She put her hand over her mouth. Maybe it was hysteria, considering all that had happened. One minute people are dying around them, the next they were making love. Of course she had no one to blame but herself for that one.

She cleared her throat and looked him dead in the

eye. "I know why I'm here. You were the one who made the offer, but I was the one who made the decision to accept it."

He shook his head. Despite everything, she found herself admiring his handsome face. Even now, little waves of completion still washed through her just looking at him.

"That's not what I mean."

She crossed her arms over her chest. Her nipples, still hard from his touch, rasped against the lace of her bra. "What is it that you mean then?"

He scrubbed a hand over his face and leveled his gaze on hers. "Mission Recovery set you up."

She made a face. "Set me up? That's impossible. You said—"

"I know what I said." He swallowed, hard. She watched the smooth movement of muscle beneath tanned skin.

"You said that guy Sanchez killed your partner and that Mission Recovery needed me because I was a dead ringer for her." No pun intended, she realized belatedly.

"That part's all true."

A tiny inkling of something cold stole into her, but she pushed it away—didn't want to feel it. She flung her arms outward in exasperation, then braced them on her hips in surrender. "Okay, you've lost me here. What in the world are you trying to say?"

"There's a group in Mission Recovery called Forward Research." He shrugged halfheartedly or maybe disdainfully, she wasn't sure which. "Their job is to find and recruit the right people for our organization."

A recruitment branch. Even the Army had one. She didn't see the problem.

"When they find a person with just the right skills they go after them," he said. "You entered the prison system and your name was flagged, your skills noted."

Made sense so far. She was very good at her job. Her only crime had been trusting Jeff. Though she still didn't get the bottom line. Maybe Logan had a problem thinking clearly after sex. Her gaze raked his body. She sure did. She wanted more. And that was not the responsible way to feel. Getting too attached to this guy would be a big mistake.

Yeah, right.

Like she hadn't already.

He matched her stance, bracing his hands on his hips. "Sometimes the new recruits need motivation. You know, incentive."

Now he had her attention. That dread she'd felt earlier made an abrupt reappearance. "And? What would this have to do with me?"

"They knew you'd need incentive."

She searched his face, his eyes. "Incentive for what?"

"To risk your life…to do something totally out of character."

She laughed again, but it came out more like a choked sigh. "What kind of incentive? I mean I'd never heard of you people until that night when the guard roused me from my cell."

"When Forward Research discovered you, they wanted you. Not necessarily at that moment, but at some point. You had the kind of advanced skills they look for. Jess's unfortunate death just happened to make your name pop up on the wrong computer screen a little earlier than anticipated. You had the skills... you had the look...they had the mission."

She waved him on. "I'm with you so far, but didn't I know most of this already?"

He nodded. "Pretty much."

She huffed a frustrated breath. "Okay, Logan, just spit it out. It's not like we've got all year here. What is it that I don't know? How was I set up?"

Logan didn't want to tell her. He didn't want to see that vulnerable innocence turn to hatred, to regret for what had just happened between them. He shouldn't have made love to her with this lie standing between them. If he'd only told her before...but it was too late for "ifs" now.

"The guard, the inmate." Her expression fell. His chest tightened. "That was Forward Research. They wanted you more receptive to any upcoming requirements. The fact that one came up when it did was just a coincidence. They discovered the evidence to clear you at the start, but they waited until you were needed. It was their ace in the hole."

She gave her head a little shake of denial. "I don't believe you."

Her voice sounded hollow, thin. The hurt in her eyes was almost more than he could bear. "It's true.

It was the only way they could ensure you'd cooperate when the time came.''

Her hands began to tremble and he wanted desperately to reach out to her…but she'd only reject him. "They put me through weeks of hell. Of fear," she said angrily. "Just to make sure I'd say yes when you asked for help?"

He nodded.

"And you!" She took a step toward him. "You've known all of this from the beginning?"

"That's right." He had to tell her every thing. "Even the handcuffs that night. That was my idea. I knew the cuffs would serve as another little prod of inducement."

She trembled with fury…with hurt. Hurt that he had caused. "You couldn't have told me?" She blinked furiously.

God, don't let her cry, he prayed.

"It's not like I was going anywhere." She flung the words at him.

He tried to take a deep breath, it caught. "I made a mistake. I should have told you…before. I—"

She held up a hand to stop him. "I don't want to talk anymore. Esteban's waiting." She turned her back on him and climbed into the waiting car.

She was right. Esteban was waiting. He would be outraged. But nothing he could say or do would get to Logan the way this had. Nothing.

THE FLIGHT BACK to Colombia was silent. Hector would only cross himself every time he looked at Logan. And Erin wasn't speaking at all.

Logan tried to analyze his feelings. Some of them were alien to him. He'd dedicated most of his life to his career. He'd never considered that maybe he should take stock of what he might be missing. He was only thirty-five. A wife and kids could come later.

But he'd never thought about either of those things until Erin Bailey came into his life. He glanced at the woman sitting as far away from him as possible. She made him yearn for things he didn't know how to describe. She made him want to come home to one woman when a mission was over. And that woman was her. But it would never work, even if he'd read correctly what he saw in her eyes when they made love. She would never understand or agree with his world. She was one of those regular people who preferred to believe that people like him only existed in the movies or in novels.

He wasn't real to her. Just a passing nightmare, one, that if they were both lucky, would be over very soon.

Still, he'd seen a spark of emotion in her eyes when they made love that warmed him to the core of his being. Something that tugged at him like nothing else ever had before.

Though it was doubtful he would live to pursue it.

Esteban was waiting.

They arrived back at the compound just over one hour later than planned. Esteban would be simmering impatiently, ready to blow up and rain down that fury on someone.

And that someone was going to be Logan. Alone.

"Go to our quarters and wait," he told Erin. He didn't want her anywhere near when Esteban blew.

She shook her head. "This was my assignment, too."

"I said—"

"I don't care what you said." She spun away from him and followed Hector who'd already headed for the house.

Logan swore hotly, repeatedly. She was too damned hardheaded for her own good.

As he'd expected, Esteban was pacing in anticipation of their return. He was not a happy camper.

"Where is my money?" he demanded.

Hector placed the two briefcases containing the cash on the floor next to Esteban's desk.

His face was red with fury. "I will have a complete accounting of your time as to why you have arrived more than one hour late. Where are the Watterses?"

"Larry and Sheila are dead," Logan said bluntly. "The four men who brought the money are dead."

Esteban's face went from red to a stroke-level purple. "What is the meaning of this? What have you done?"

"We still have the coke in our possession. If your people in California want to set up another meet, I'll personally escort it to them."

Esteban took two slow, deep breaths. "You will tell me from the beginning how this happened."

Logan held his ground. "There's nothing to tell.

The meet went sour. People are dead. It's done. There isn't anything else to tell.''

From the corner of his eye, Logan saw Hector cross himself again.

''Do you have a death wish, Mr. Logan Wilks?'' Esteban demanded as he reached for the 9 mm he kept on his desk. ''For I do not tolerate acts of insubordination.''

''One of the guys,'' Erin said, her voice sounding small yet abrupt amid the harsh male voices still echoing in the room. ''He tried to make a pass at me and I shot him. It went downhill from there. Sheila and Larry fought to the death to save your money.''

Logan wanted to reach out and snatch back those words. What the hell did she mean taking the blame away from him? Didn't she know—?

Esteban's savage gaze shifted to her. ''*You* caused this unnecessary havoc?'' Disbelief muscled its way to the surface of his expression.

She lifted her chin and glared right back at him. ''A man grabs my ass and refuses to let go, he's going to eat a bullet. Isn't that what you taught me?''

''This is my—''

Esteban held up a hand and halted what Logan would have said. ''This man, did you kill him with the first shot?''

Erin smiled. ''Right between the eyes.''

Logan watched in morbid fascination as she put on an Academy Award winning performance. He didn't know whether to kiss her or kill her.

Esteban uttered a strained laugh. Then laughed some more. He laughed until he had to stop and catch his breath. "This is a truly remarkable story!" He turned to Cortez. "Is this not remarkable, my loyal friend?"

Cortez nodded. "Most remarkable."

Equal parts relief and irritation washed over Logan. When he got her outside…

"I shall call my friends in California and warn them that the next men they send to do business had better not be ass grabbers."

Esteban and Cortez laughed. So did Hector. Logan simply couldn't work up the enthusiasm. Erin only smiled, far too seductively. Was this payback? Didn't she realize she was risking too much here?

"Logan, your wife is very good," Esteban remarked. "Is she not?"

Logan managed a tight smile for Esteban, then for Erin. "Truer words have never been spoken, my friend." He turned back to Esteban. "She's amazing."

Esteban's smile vanished. "All of you, go. I will speak to this amazing woman alone."

Cortez and Hector started for the door. Logan didn't move.

Esteban arrowed a challenging gaze at him. "You have a problem, my friend Logan?"

"She's my wife. I don't want her punished for my failure to see that the mission was accomplished."

Esteban laughed loudly again. "You have no worries, Logan. I have no plans to punish your lovely wife. I simply wish to convey private words to her."

Fury roared inside Logan. He would not leave without Erin.

She turned to him. "Logan, go. I'll be there in a minute."

Logan sent one final look of warning in Esteban's direction. "I'll be waiting right outside."

"As you wish," Esteban said smugly.

When the door closed behind Logan, Erin steeled herself for whatever Esteban intended. She didn't want to die. But she wanted even less to see Logan killed. If Esteban required services of her in exchange for going easy on Logan, she was prepared to perform. After all, would there be much difference between that and what she'd done with Logan just hours ago?

Tears threatened to well in her eyes at the thought. Yes, there was a monumental difference. Unfortunately. She was in love with Logan. This man—she stared directly at Esteban—was a menace to society. He didn't deserve to live and if her body was the price of seeing that Logan got the goods to bring him down. So be it.

"Sit, please." Esteban gestured to the leather-tufted wing chair before his desk. "Would you like something to drink? You must be thirsty after such an ordeal."

She took the seat he offered. "Yes. Make it a double." She'd always wanted to say that. God knew she probably wouldn't ever have the chance again.

While she watched, Esteban poured her a drink and handed it to her. He settled in the adjacent chair. "My sister is very impressed with you, Sara."

Erin gulped a big swallow of the liquor and grimaced as it flowed down her throat. "I'm very impressed with her as well," she croaked, then cleared her throat.

Esteban chuckled. "She likes you. This is a rare phenomena when one considers the sort of friends I must keep for doing business."

Erin nodded. "I can understand that." Though she regretted Sheila was dead, there definitely was no love lost between them.

"Then you also understand how important it is to nurture this relationship."

Another swallow slid down Erin's throat. She didn't grimace this time. The liquor went down considerably more smoothly. "I'm good with that. Maria's terrific. Is there something in particular you want me to do?"

"You realize that you owe me a great debt now, do you not?"

Erin stilled, her pulse tripped as anxiety resurrected inside her. "Yes. I do."

"In return for my overlooking today's fiasco you will watch my sister for me." He made a hopeful gesture. "Sometimes a member of one's family can become a burden of sorts. You would keep me informed as to what she is doing at all times. Until I make my decision."

Erin frowned. This whole conversation had her confused. "What decision?"

Esteban looked directly into her eyes. "On how you will kill her for me."

HE WAS GOING IN.

Logan had waited outside long enough. He wouldn't risk one more second. He strode toward the door, not caring what the guard said, his pace increasing the closer he got. Erin was in there, Logan was going after her. The SUV they had returned in still sat in front of the house, keys in the ignition. He knew what he had to do. But first he had to get her out of the house.

The front door suddenly opened and she stepped out into the dim glow spilling from the overhead terrace lights.

Logan double-timed it to her position and snagged her by the arm. He headed into the shadows made by the trees, out of sight, out of hearing distance of anyone who might be attempting to listen.

Though relieved to see her in one piece and apparently unharmed, he was beyond furious.

"I don't know what made you do something so incredibly stupid," he said from between clenched teeth, "but I'm taking you out of here tonight. Now."

She tried to pull free of his grasp. "I won't go."

He glowered at her, for the good it did in the dark. "Are you completely crazy? What the hell kind of stunt was that?" His fingers tightened around her arms as renewed fury whipped through him at his next thought. "What did you have to promise him for getting me off the hook?"

"Let me go."

He was hurting her. She didn't have to say it…his fingers were closed around her arms like vises. Damn. He released her and exhaled a shaky breath.

"I have to get you out of here. It's not safe for you anymore."

"It was never safe," she countered, her voice far too calm.

Something was very wrong. He could feel it.

"And that little stunt I pulled probably saved your life, thank you very much."

"Don't expect me to thank you," he said tightly. "You took too great a risk. You—"

"Did what had to be done," she cut in. "The *mission* above all else. Isn't that what you taught me?"

He clenched his jaw hard and counted to three. When he could speak in a reasonable tone again he went on, "I'm taking you out tonight. I'll deal with Esteban. You're out of this as of right now "

"No."

If he had to carry her out, he would. But that would draw attention, he didn't want that. "Why in God's name would you want to stay? I'm giving you a get-out-of-jail free card. You can leave now. You're through, *finito*."

"I have to find a way to save his sister."

This just kept getting better and better. "What the hell does she have to do with any of this?"

"He's going to have her murdered. I have to help her."

Logan grappled for control of his runaway emotions. How did he get this through her head? "You have to go. *Tonight*. Besides, how do you know he's going to kill his sister?"

The silence went on for what felt like an eternity.

"Because he wants me to do the job for him."

Chapter Thirteen

Erin was awake before sunrise. She lay very still. She didn't want to wake Logan, though she wasn't sure he was actually asleep. His breathing was deep and even and he hadn't moved a muscle, but she couldn't be absolutely certain.

She wasn't sure of anything anymore.

Logan's people had set her up for this. Made her feel afraid and vulnerable, just so she'd do their bidding—had evidence that would absolve her. Anger unfurled inside her. Why would anyone purposely cause another human being to experience what she had those last few weeks in prison? It was just so unbelievable that the *good* guys would do such a thing. But they had.

She wanted to hate them for that.

She really did.

But somehow she couldn't. Deep down she knew for certain that she would never have agreed to do this if she hadn't had incentive. She almost laughed at how foolish she'd been back then. Just a few short weeks ago. Erin Bailey played by the rules. She never made trouble for anyone. She was a good girl.

Had life in prison been tolerable, she'd have done her time and never complained. Sure the idea of getting her life back and seeing Jeff pay for what he'd done would have been alluring, but not alluring enough. Erin had spent a lifetime being a by-the-book kind of person.

That person no longer existed.

She'd seen too much. Realized how petty her problems were in the overall scheme of things. There were people like Logan who died every day to make sure people like her were safe and could live their lives the way they chose.

As angry as she was at Logan and Mission Recovery, she could never look at things the way she had before. Things simply weren't black and white. There was lots of gray. And she was in the middle of about the grayest moment she'd dreamed could exist.

She would see this thing through. She would not turn her back on Logan—could not. She loved him, dammit. Their lovemaking, scandalous as it was in the back seat of that limo, had sealed her fate, physically and mentally. Of course, she understood that he didn't love her, that a woman like her wasn't in his plans. And that was okay, she would live with it. Well, maybe it wasn't okay, but she would learn to live with it. No matter what she thought she read in his eyes or in any action he had taken since this whole thing started, it was all about the mission for him. Yesterday didn't change anything. In fact, he'd tried to get her to stop.

He had wanted her physically, but that was all.

She still wanted him. No matter how angry he'd made her. No matter that he would never love her...

Enough, she ordered silently. She might have thrown Esteban's suspicions off track last night, but she was not stupid. The driver or someone who just happened to oversee what really happened could blow their cover. Suspicious or not, Esteban would be watching them closely now. She had to focus...to play the game.

It was the only way to cheat death. To rescue Esteban's sister.

To help Logan accomplish the mission.

POUNDING ON THE DOOR snapped Logan from his own worrisome thoughts. He was pretty sure Erin was awake, but she'd remained quiet, so he had, too. They were both up now.

He grabbed his weapon and tugged on his jeans, stumbling toward the door as he did. He flipped the light switch and jerked the door open. "What?"

It was Cortez.

"There is a briefing in five minutes."

"We'll be there."

Cortez stared pointedly at him. "Only you."

Logan swore silently as he watched the man amble away. He slammed the door and plowed his fingers through his hair. What now? There weren't any runs scheduled for a couple of days. Tension coiled inside him. What was Esteban up to? Had he found out what really happened in L.A.? If he intended to execute Logan this morning, that would leave Erin at his mercy. Logan had to find a way to get her out of here.

Logan turned to find her waiting in the bedroom door, fear etched across her face.

"What's going on?"

"I don't know." He wanted to say so much more, but couldn't.

"I'll get dressed."

"No need. He only wants me."

Her gaze connected fully with his. He saw the worry there. "Fine, I'll take a shower then."

"Fine," he said stiffly.

She crooked a finger for him to follow her. As he did, she snagged a writing pen from the dresser and then went into the bathroom. She turned on the shower and sat down on the closed toilet lid. After tearing off a long section of white toilet paper, she started writing.

She offered him the note. He took it, their fingers brushed, sending an electrical charge straight to his loins, clenching his gut. He flinched before he could stop himself. The note read: *Don't go! What if he plans to kill you?*

He took the pen from her and scribbled his response.

I have to go. You know that. Keep your head down. I WILL be back for you.

She shook her head adamantly when she read the note, then started writing again. *DON'T GO!* she penned in huge letters.

He just looked at her. She knew he had no choice.

Her hands were shaking now, but she wrote furiously. When she handed the note to him tears were brimming in her eyes. God, he wanted to hold her. To promise her it would be all right. He blinked, startled by the strength of his own emotions.

He stared down at her handwriting. *Swear to me that you'll come back. Swear that you won't let him kill you.*

He crumpled the toilet paper. So many feelings bombarded him at once that he couldn't sort them...couldn't understand.

She pushed up, forced him to look her in the eye, took the paper from him and placed his right hand over her heart and then waited for his response.

He stared into those shimmering violet eyes, felt the beating of her heart beneath his palm and knew that no matter what it took, he would be back for her. He pulled her into his arms, held her tighter than he ever had before. He felt her tremble...or maybe it was him.

He pressed his lips to her ear, "I swear I will be back for you."

He kissed her hard and fast, then walked out. He grabbed a shirt and his shoes on the way to the door. He didn't look back. Knew better than to look back.

One backward glance and he'd never be able to leave her.

Erin stood in the bedroom doorway, the crumpled length of toilet paper in her hand, and watched him go.

Her heart raced in her chest. She had to find Maria

and try to figure out what Esteban was up to this morning. Maybe, together, they could escape and somehow help Logan.

Erin turned off the shower, then ripped the paper into smaller lengths, rewadded each piece and flushed them down the toilet. She had to hurry. She finger-combed her hair and pulled on some clothes.

First up, she had to find Maria.

OVER HALF AN HOUR had passed and Erin hadn't been able to locate Maria.

Logan had left in the SUV with Hector and Carlos. Erin had watched from one corner of the garden wall. All appeared to be in order. Logan was armed. She'd seen the butt of the weapon protruding from his waist-band at the small of his back. That was a good sign, wasn't it?

Then again the Caldarone brothers could gang up on him. She sighed wearily. Okay, one thing at time.

Maria wasn't in her garden, but then it was early, it hadn't been daylight an hour yet. She had to be in the house somewhere.

So, Erin would go in. If she ran into Esteban, she would simply say that she was hoping to have break-fast with Maria to get to know her better. Hadn't Esteban asked her to nurture the relationship?

That was the ticket. She had a perfect excuse to be looking for his sister, despite the early hour.

The house was eerily quiet. Thankfully her sneakers were silent on the extravagant marble floor. Maria's room would not be on the first floor, Erin knew the layout pretty well now, but she would check just in case.

All the rooms, including the terrace out back, were empty. She had to go upstairs. Pausing at the bottom of the staircase to take a couple of bolstering breaths, Erin dug way down deep for every ounce of courage she possessed.

She could do this.

She climbed the stairs slowly, the lush runner keeping her footfalls silent. When she reached the second story landing, she considered her options. Esteban's private room was to the right, the east wing of the house. Maria's was likely in the west wing.

She moved quietly down the carpeted hall. She eased open each door she passed. A couple of guest bedrooms which were empty. At the end of the corridor was a set of double doors, much like those that led to Esteban's suite. This had to be Maria's suite.

Erin paused outside the door. Drew in another breath of courage and reached for the door handle. Her hand shook. She clenched her fist and struggled to keep it together. Silence screaming around her, she ordered herself to calm. She reached for the door handle and opened the door. It swung inward without so much as a creak.

The large sitting room was empty. Quiet as a tomb. But Erin was sure anyone within fifty feet of her could hear her heart pounding.

Holding her breath, she eased into the semi-dark room. A table lamp threw out enough light for her to see her way around. She closed the door behind her with a *click* that seemed to echo like a shotgun blast.

When no one came rushing into the room or no alarms wailed, she allowed herself to breathe.

Like Esteban's, the sitting room was large and elegantly furnished, a bit more femininely, of course. Erin moved toward the bedroom door. Maybe Maria was still asleep.

As she passed the intricately carved mahogany desk, something snagged her attention. Erin paused, studying the items on the desk. A personal computer system. Papers, books, headphones that were attached to a rather elaborate-looking tape or CD player. Erin rubbed her forehead, hoping to erase the insistent ache there. Nothing so unusual. Lights on the CD/tape player flickered once, twice, then the bar of lights hovered at midrange, finally dimming. Music. Maria must have left it on when she went to bed.

When Erin would have turned away, the title of one of the books drew her gaze back. Her heart bumped against her rib cage. She knew that title, had one back home in storage just like it. One of the top hackers on the planet had written that book. What did Maria know about hacking? Or need to know?

Curiosity overriding all else, Erin leaned down and switched on the brass desk lamp. She skimmed the papers scattered on the desk. Stared at pictures of herself and Logan. Erin pivoted abruptly to stare at the books on the shelves behind her. Dread sank into her bones. Every book, every software program—she turned back to the computer system on the desk, nudged the mouse to shut down the screen saver, allowing a blue screen filled with icons to appear—every electronic tool one would need to break into any system that existed was there.

Her thoughts oddly still, she focused on the details. The system had two hard drives. One for the Net; one for files. Files the owner didn't want exposed to the cyber world, to the possibility of a security breach.

The flickering lights drew her attention once more. Her fingers numb with fear and disbelief, Erin reached for the headphones. She pressed one side to her ear. Her voice. Magnified so loud she almost flinched. Feigned cries of ecstasy and Esteban's name...urging him on when he actually lay passed out on the bed. The undeniable click of computer keys.

Erin slowly laid the headphones back on the desk.

This couldn't be.

She shook her head in denial. Clenched her jaw in defiance. How could this be?

"I see you have discovered my secret."

Maria.

Erin turned toward the double doors that opened into the corridor. Maria stood there, fully dressed, looking as regal as ever. Coming closer, she seemed to float across the room, the epitome of grace and elegance.

"What is this?" Erin barely recognized her own voice. The sudden image of the rose with no thorns loomed large in her mind, nothing to mar its beauty. Nothing to mar this woman's...no hint of evil.

"I wanted to trust you, Sara." Maria's expression

hardened. "If that's your real name, which I doubt. But you let me down. You're even worse than the others."

Erin shook her head. "What do you have to do with this?" She gestured, confused, to the papers on the desk...the books, then turned to the woman. "Who are you?"

Maria lifted her chin and stared directly into Erin's eyes. "I am the one who makes everything happen."

It took a moment for Erin to absorb the ramifications of that statement. Before she could regroup, Maria went on.

"I have the contacts. I make the rules. *I* make the decisions. Esteban is merely a figurehead, shall we say."

"But why?" Erin couldn't grasp the concept. "Why be so secretive? Why not run the show openly?"

Maria sniffed rather indelicately. "In this male dominated, macho society? You must be joking? Or perhaps, like most Americans, you are simply naïve. Women are not permitted such respect. No one would take me seriously...certainly they would not take orders from me."

Dear Lord. This was why Esteban had never been caught. He simply did what his sister told him. She had the contacts, she'd said. No one could finger him because he wasn't involved on that level. She did the traveling, made the contacts. All under the guise of buying flowers.

"Ingenious, no?" Maria suggested, as if she'd read Erin's mind.

Oh, yes, very ingenious. "This gave us away?" She pointed to the headphones and the recording.

"Unfortunately, yes." Maria shook her head. "It concerns me greatly that the two of you slipped under our security net. We are usually much more cautious."

"You've known all this time?"

"Not until early this morning," Maria said candidly. "Cortez was the first to note that the recording sounded somewhat forced. So I listened for myself." She laughed softly. "I have listened to my brother's distasteful performances before, you were most definitely acting."

Great, this was her fault.

"That alone was not enough to sway me, however." Maria moved closer still. "Out of curiosity, I had the tape magnified again and again until this last time I heard clearly the sound of typing."

She paused only inches from Erin and shook her head slowly from side to side. "And then the grind of files being downloaded onto disk. I knew what you'd done—for the good it did you. There is nothing on Esteban's computer, because he is nothing."

A new kind of fear snaked around Erin's chest. "Where's Logan?"

Maria smiled. "Ah, your husband. Not to worry, he isn't dead yet. He is being taken to one of our close friends. A man who served Castro for many years as his intelligence officer. A man who now serves me. He will extract all relevant information from Logan and then he will kill him." Maria glanced at the gold wristwatch she wore and sighed. "He has some time yet, I am certain. Unless, of course, he breaks more quickly than estimated."

Erin had to stop this somehow.

"Venido!"

On Maria's command, two guards rushed into the room.

"Now," Maria said to her. "Let us see what you know."

HECTOR HAD INSISTED that Logan drive.

Logan was unfamiliar with the route they'd instructed him to take, but then he'd expected to be. Esteban had ordered the three of them to check out a couple of his factories and Logan had not been privy to their locations as of yet. Esteban had gone on to explain that several reports of incidents at the cocaine processing facilities had prompted him to make this unscheduled inspection.

Logan wasn't buying it. Something was going down, and it likely included executing him. He hoped like hell Erin would stay clear of Esteban until Logan could dump his silent partners.

The brooding Caldarone brothers looked about as happy as Logan felt, but he was sure it was for totally different reasons.

"Turn left here," Hector said abruptly, almost waiting too late for Logan to make the turn.

He cut the SUV hard to the left. Spanish curses accompanied the two men's attempts to stay upright.

Logan decided to use their careless habits to his advantage. Unlike him, neither of his two passengers wore their seat belts. Gain some speed, slam on the brakes, throw Hector against the windshield and try to put a bullet in him and his brother before one of them did it to him first. Sounded like a good plan to Logan.

"Slow down, you fool!" Carlos shouted from the back seat. "This road is treacherous."

"There is another turn—"

Glass shattered. Mid-sentence, Hector slumped forward onto the dash.

Logan glanced at the bullet hole in the windshield and the spiderweb of broken glass around it.

"What the hell?" he muttered. Maybe Esteban had decided to kill three birds with one stone, so to speak.

"Faster," Carlos screamed, obviously no longer concerned with the ruggedness of the road. "Find some cover!"

Another bullet piercing glass sounded right behind Logan. Carlos collapsed into the seat. Logan swore and pushed the SUV for all it was worth. If Esteban wanted them all dead, why hadn't he saved time and done it himself at the briefing?

A dark figure stepped into the road just ahead. Logan braced for a hard swerve.

Ferrelli.

Logan skidded to a stop mere inches from the cocky son of a bitch. He should have known from the perfect hits that it was Ferrelli.

Ferrelli rounded the hood; jerked the passenger side

door open and dragged Hector out, then climbed into the seat next to Logan.

"I think you're taking this angel gig a bit too seriously, Ferrelli. I barely stopped this thing in time."

"You've been made," Ferrelli explained, ignoring the jab. "Tech Ops intercepted a cellular telephone call from Esteban to a nasty fellow named Cruz. One of Castro's former cohorts. These jokers—" he hitched a thumb toward Carlos in the back seat "—were taking you to Cruz for a little intense one-on-one interrogation."

Logan rammed the gearshift into Reverse and punched the accelerator to the floor.

Ferrelli braced himself. "Backup's on the way. We're supposed to rendezvous with them at—"

"There's no time." Reaching a wide enough spot in the road, Logan hit the brakes hard, doing a 180-degree skidding turn. "We have to get Erin out of there."

Ferrelli held his gaze during the fraction of a second it took the SUV to lunge forward after Logan stomped the gas pedal. "We may be too late. If we aren't, getting past the guards without alerting Esteban will be tricky. May even do more harm than good."

"I'm going back," Logan repeated. *"Now."*

Chapter Fourteen

With Carlos strapped into the front passenger seat and Ferrelli lounging low in the back, the gate to Esteban's compound opened without hesitation when Logan neared. Apparently not everyone had been briefed as to Logan's new standing with their leader.

Logan sped through the gate and parked near the guest house. As he'd feared it would be, it was empty. With both his weapon and Carlos's, Logan had all the firepower he would need. Like all Specialists, Ferrelli was prepared as well.

"There's two at the gate, six patrolling the grounds and another two around here somewhere," Logan explained quietly as he scanned the perimeter around their position for any movement. "I'm going in after Erin. Esteban's personal bodyguard and a couple of the guards I mentioned may be inside."

"It'll be just like taking candy from babies," Ferrelli assured him.

Logan nodded and headed toward the house, careful to maintain cover at all times. He didn't have to worry about odds, whether it was five to one or twenty to one, Ferrelli would manage. All Specialists had extensive stealth and sniper training. They were the cream of the crop—made the elite Navy SEALs look like Boy Scouts. Specialists did the jobs no one else could.

Silence greeted Logan when he entered the house from the rear terrace. Not making a sound, he moved deeper into the dimly lit interior. The kitchen and dining room were empty. So was Esteban's office, the briefing room and the front parlor. That left the upstairs.

Logan moved silently to the bottom of the staircase. Just as he lifted his right foot to take the first step up, the click of a weapon engaging echoed behind him.

Logan froze.

"Coming back was not a smart move." Cortez reached around and plucked the weapon from Logan's raised hand. The barrel of Cortez's weapon bored into Logan's skull. "But now that you are here, you might as well join the party."

"I've always liked parties," Logan said wryly, thankful for the moment that Cortez hadn't had the foresight to pat him down. Carlos's weapon was tucked into Logan's waistband. He'd purposely pulled his T-shirt loose in front to drape over it.

Cortez urged him up the stairs. "I think your lovely wife likes this party as well."

Logan gritted his teeth against the desire to turn around and tear the man apart, but that would be a mistake. Getting shot now wouldn't help Erin. He'd sworn he'd come back for her. No way was he letting her down.

He would make his move when the time was right. Logan took the final step up to the landing.

And the time was right *now*.

He whirled around, simultaneously drawing the weapon. When Cortez prepared to pull off a shot, Logan jammed a foot into his midsection, sending him tumbling down the stairs. Cortez's shot went high. Logan's didn't.

Logan checked out the east wing first. Nothing. Fear that he was too late tightened in his chest. He'd promised her and he'd failed.

As he neared the end of the corridor in the west wing, he heard muffled voices. He couldn't say yet if they were male or female, one or two.

He paused when he found one of the guards lying dead in an open doorway. Why would Esteban kill one of his guards? On closer inspection, Logan recognized the guard as Manuel, the one whose life Erin had saved with her quick thinking that first night. Maybe the guy had tried to return the favor.

A scream.

Erin.

Logan reached for calm. Forced himself to rely on the skills that had saved his life and the lives of others numerous times. Now was not the time for emotions or haste. He had to move cautiously.

There was a narrow crack in the door where it wasn't quite closed, but it wasn't wide enough for him to see. He could hear Esteban's enraged voice...Erin's fearful one. Logan hardened his heart against it. He couldn't help her if he acted on his emotions.

Erin sat tied to a leather swivel chair. Her lip was bleeding, her right eye swollen. A mixture of fury and fear hit Logan like a sucker punch to the gut.

"I will ask you one last time," Esteban threatened, his tone impatient, deadly. The business end of the weapon in his hand jammed against her temple. "Who sent you here?"

She stared up at him without saying a single word.

Respect welled in Logan. She was good.

No way could he spend the rest of his life without this woman.

He leveled his weapon on his target, square in the back of Esteban's head. Logan snugged his finger to the trigger—

"Drop your weapon."

It was a woman's voice.

A barrel poked Logan in the back. "Drop it now or I will kill you."

Esteban's sister.

Maria.

Esteban whipped around, his weapon still leveled on Erin. Disbelief registered on his face when his gaze locked with Logan's. "You!"

Logan's lips tightened as Maria jabbed him in the back with the weapon. "Drop your weapon or she dies now!" Maria warned.

He tossed the borrowed weapon onto the carpeted floor.

"Move!" she demanded, jabbing him again.

She was in on this, too. Erin had insisted on staying just to save this woman, only to discover *this*. Logan moved into the center of the room at Maria's continued prompting.

Erin sobbed out Logan's name.

He wanted desperately to go to her, but didn't dare make a move for fear of setting off a deadly chain reaction.

"Maybe I will have some answers now," Esteban sneered.

"Better men than you have tried interrogating me," Logan challenged. "But if you think you're up to it, have at it." He gestured to Erin. "She doesn't know anything. Let her go and try your hand with me. I'm the one who can give you what you want."

Logan tried to reassure Erin with his eyes. Tears were rolling down her cheeks but she sat up straighter, as if glad he was there. Just seeing the suffering she'd already endured made him want to kill Esteban with his bare hands.

"No, no. She stays." Esteban swaggered toward Logan, waving his gun like the madman he was. "And I believe you will talk after you see what I have in store for your lovely wife."

"Enough of your crude theatrics," Maria roared like a dragon rather than the demure woman she'd appeared to be. "*I* will extract the answers I require."

Esteban glared at her. "I! I! I!" He beat his fist against his chest. "I do all the dirty work and you," he snarled, "you do nothing but spout useless orders."

Well, well, Logan mused. There was trouble in paradise. No wonder Esteban wanted his sister dead. He was tired of being bossed around by a woman.

"Watch your step, brother dear. You would be nothing without me."

Outrage still burning in his black eyes, Esteban feigned humility. "How could I forget? You are the brains. I am the brawn." He flung an arm in Erin's direction. "Then let me do my job."

Maria's posture relaxed slightly. "Proceed," she relented.

Logan tensed, prepared to hurl himself at Esteban. He couldn't let him do this...

"Tell me who sent you," Esteban demanded of Erin once more. "Or I will destroy your lover bit by bit right before your eyes."

Erin's gaze locked with Logan's. He saw the terror there, but also an underlying determination. His tension rocketed to a new level. God, don't let her do anything foolhardy, he prayed. She turned back to Esteban and stared up at him in blatant disdain.

"You did," she said hoarsely.

Esteban slapped her. She cried out. Logan jerked forward. Maria's weapon bored more deeply into his spleen. "If you move," she warned, "I won't bother shooting you. I'll shoot her."

Logan froze. He fisted his hands in desperation. He had to stop this. Where the hell was Ferrelli?

"Who sent you?" Esteban roared as he raised his hand to strike Erin again.

She stopped him with her words. "*You did.* You sent me to kill your sister."

Esteban stiffened visibly. "What kind of nonsense is this?" He jammed the barrel of his weapon to the side of her head once more. "Confess that you are making this up!"

There was no way to miss the new thread of nervous tension in his voice.

Erin looked directly at Maria. "He said you liked me...trusted me. He wanted me to get close to you so I could keep him informed until he made up his mind how he wanted me to kill you."

"Lies! All lies!" Esteban screamed. He grabbed a handful of Erin's hair and jerked. "She is a lying whore!"

"That's why I was trying to find you today," Erin finished quickly, grimacing with the new pain. "I wanted to warn you."

"Bastardo," Maria accused, her full attention moving to Esteban. "You wanted me out of the way."

"I swear she is lying." Esteban released his hold on Erin and stumbled backward, away from the death ray aimed at him. He waved his weapon in front of him. "You know I would never hurt you, Maria."

Maria's aim swung toward Esteban. She fired before he could gather his wits and shoot or run. Logan knocked Maria's arm up when she would have pulled off another round, this one aimed right at Erin. Her shot hit the window beyond Erin. Maria spun wildly, aiming for Logan next. He flung himself at her, taking her to the floor as he went down. The weapon flew from her hand. She scrambled for it. Before she could reach it, Logan had her. A second later she was out cold.

"We're clear," Ferrelli announced. "Housekeeping is in the air."

Pushing to his feet, Logan glared at Ferrelli who stood in the open doorway grinning widely. "'Bout time you showed up."

"What can I say?" Ferrelli chuckled. "I didn't want to steal your glory."

Logan nodded toward Maria. "Secure her."

"Will do."

Logan bounded across the room and dropped to his knees before Erin. He quickly dispensed with her bonds. Ferrelli was saying something, but Logan wasn't listening. All that mattered to him right now was that Erin was safe.

She went straight into his arms. "I told you I'd be back," he murmured.

She exhaled a shaky breath. "I never doubted you for a moment."

Logan helped her to her feet. "Let's get out of here."

As the adrenaline receded and fear of what could have happened took hold, another kind of reality set in. This was the end of their time together.

The mission was over.

Erin would go back to her life now.

His arm tightened instinctively around her. For the first time in his life he understood the true meaning of needing someone so desperately that he couldn't survive without that person.

Without Erin.

How could he ever let her go?

But how could he ask her to stay?

ERIN AND LOGAN were immediately flown to D.C. for what he called a "debriefing." Erin had already told him and Ferrelli everything Maria had told her. Though not forthcoming herself, Maria's computer contained everything they were looking for and more, dates, names, *everything*. Including the fact that Maria had set up a number of aliases operating out of Venezuela, Brazil and Mexico.

Her Brazilian alias proved most intriguing, as well as telling. She'd been having an affair with a high-level military official for years. He never once suspected her duplicity. She had used her time with him to gain access to his computer system. Considering the top-notch hacker she was, the rest had been a piece of cake.

Technical Operations had their work cut out for them now, analyzing all the data and determining where all the stolen weapons had ended up. The Drug Enforcement Agency would take over the closing down of Esteban's drug operation. Including the arrest of all those present at Esteban's party a few nights ago.

The mission was a success.

And it was over.

Erin paced the room she'd been assigned for the night. She'd showered already, but she couldn't sleep. Her thoughts keep going to the way Logan had held her after Esteban was dead. As if he feared she might disappear. She couldn't stop thinking about the way he'd come back for her even knowing the risk involved. Ferrelli had told her how Logan had refused to wait for backup.

She sank onto the edge of the bed. And then there was the way he'd made love to her. Surely she couldn't have been that mistaken about his feelings for her. There was definitely no mistaking her own. She stared at the place where the gold band had resided on her left ring finger. It lay on the dresser across the room now. It was just part of the cover...part of the act. It had all been an act.

The last two weeks were what Logan lived for. His career as a specialist was his life. *The mission.* He'd said as much himself. He didn't want a wife. Especially not one who wasn't a part of his world. What would she do while he was away on a life-and-death mission, sit home and bake brownies? She couldn't live like that. Not once had he given her the first impression that he wanted the house and white picket fence anyway.

He did have feelings for her. That much she was certain of. But those feelings would never be enough to bond a relationship this shaky. He would never be happy in her world. And his current one didn't exactly promote the marriage and family ideal.

The best thing Erin could do for Logan, as well as herself, was to say goodbye. And to walk away. She wouldn't tell him how she felt.

He would never know how hard she'd fallen.

It would be the best for all concerned.

LOGAN PUNCHED his pillow again, but it didn't help. There would be no sleep tonight. But then, how could he sleep? Erin was just a few doors down. He wanted to be with her. To make love to her again. To prove to her, as well as to himself, that it was real...not just some stress-induced infatuation.

But that couldn't happen.

Although Erin had performed above and beyond the call of duty, this was not the life for her. She would have her own safe little haven in Atlanta where no one would be shooting at her or trying to beat information out of her.

How could he ask her to wait for him between missions? That would be too cruel for words. She deserved better than that. He expelled a defeated breath. He might as well face it, Erin was better off without him. He knew it. And there couldn't be any question in her mind—not after those last few hours of enduring Esteban's torture.

Letting go would be the best for all concerned.

After the briefing tomorrow morning. He would simply say goodbye and walk away.

A new thought occurred to him. He shook his head. No, it would never work. He chewed his lip...well maybe it could. Hope swelled in his chest. It might just work.

There was only one way to find out.

HER BACK STIFF with the tension dancing up her spine, Erin sat in one of the two chairs facing Lucas Camp's desk. Logan occupied the other.

He'd been cordial to her—polite, professional—as if nothing had happened.

She wanted to scream!

But it would be pointless. Hadn't she risked her heart for a man before? And where had it gotten her? She wasn't going to go out on that limb again. She was far enough into shaky territory as it was.

Lucas had updated them on the ongoing events at Esteban's estate. Now owned with the Colombian government's blessing, lock, stock and barrel, by the United States government. The seized assets would amount to millions that could, in turn, be used to bring down others like Esteban and Maria and to help the street children in Colombia. Erin had to admit that she felt a certain pride at knowing she'd helped make that happen, but losing her heart wasn't part of the bargain.

"Excellent work, Erin." Lucas smiled at her. "You performed a great service for your country."

"Thank you," she managed, her voice as stiff as her posture.

"I'm sure it will please you to know that Jeff Monteberry was indicted three days ago and the charges against you have been erased from all files." He passed an envelope to her. "It contains all the pertinent paperwork. You're free to resume your life as if none of this ever happened."

Erin took the envelope, her hands shaking. The elation she'd fully expected to feel didn't come. Jeff was getting his and she was free—for real. And, she was alive. Pretty damned good considering what she'd been through. That was all fine, but...

"Congratulations."

Erin glanced at Logan. A fleeting glance was all she dared. But even in that small space of time he gifted her with a little smile that yanked hard on her heartstrings. "Thank you," she managed, her voice shaking as badly as her hands. She would never see him again.

This was it.

The end.

"There's just one other thing," Lucas ventured. "Logan tells me that you're a crackerjack undercover agent."

Forcing her attention back to Lucas, Erin made a choking sound that she hoped passed for a laugh. A familiar kind of heat funneled inside her with the knowledge that Logan was watching her. But she couldn't look at him again, it was just too hard. "I muddled through if that's what you mean." She squared her shoulders. "I was lucky."

"Oh you did more than muddle through," Lucas countered. "In fact, I believe you would be an asset to this organization." He inclined his head and studied her more closely. "That is if you're looking for a job."

The offer rattled her. Had Logan said that many good things about her? Why would he do that? A whirlwind of thoughts knitted her brow into a worried frown. Confusion reigned as she turned Lucas's words over in her head.

Was this spy stuff really for her? She relented and

glanced at the man sitting next to her. That dark, dark gaze collided with hers and she shivered, felt the power of him all the way to her toes. She quickly turned back to Lucas. She had to pay attention...to think.

"I'm not sure I'd be right for this kind of life," she said in all honesty.

Lucas nodded. "I understand." He sighed. "But I certainly hate to lose Logan."

Erin's frown deepened, eliciting the beginnings of a stress headache. What was the man talking about? She looked from one to the other, then back to Lucas. "Why would you lose Logan?"

Lucas shrugged. "He insists that if you walk away so will he." A ghost of a smile lifted one corner of Lucas's mouth. "It seems you had an *effect* on him."

Afraid to believe her ears, but equally terrified not to, Erin turned in her seat to face Logan. "Is that true? Are you really willing to give it all up for me?"

"In a heartbeat."

If the sincerity in his tone hadn't told her, the absolute finality in his eyes would have. Happiness bloomed in her chest. *This was real.* No more make-believe.

Her mind spun with questions and possibilities. She didn't know where to begin making a decision like this. She pressed a hand to her chest as if it might slow the racing of her heart. Logan took that hand in his and squeezed. His touch or the way he looked at her, or maybe both crystallized the moment, made everything as clear as glass. She loved him. Her life was with him, wherever that took her.

"On one condition," she said to Lucas.

He lifted a questioning eyebrow.

"That Logan and I be teamed together. We're on-the-job partners or no deal."

"I'm afraid it's not that simple," Lucas informed her solemnly. "There's a more far-reaching condition involved."

Erin's hopes fell. "I don't understand."

"You'll have to ask Logan that one, it's his condition," Lucas informed her.

She shot to her feet and glowered down at Logan. Here she was dancing out on that limb and he was holding out on her. "What the hell do you mean getting my hopes up like that and then shattering them in the next breath?" She could barely stand the ache in her chest. How could he do this?

He stood and looked squarely at her. "It's a little complicated. You see, I realized I don't want just an on-the-job partner. I want a wife. A *real* one." He smiled that sexy, crooked grin that took her breath. "Yes is the only acceptable answer."

Myriad emotions rushed through her, but one rose above all others—love. She threw her arms around his neck and hugged him tight. "Yes!" She drew back suddenly and frowned petulantly at him. "But only if you kiss me right now."

Logan obliged. Erin intended to see that he spent the rest of his life doing just that.

"Thank God," Lucas Camp said with obvious relief. "If you two can slow down just a minute we'll talk about your next assignment."

"After the honeymoon," Logan said between kisses.

Erin knew for certain then and there that she, not the mission, would always come first to the man she loved.

* * * * *

*Next month, make sure you pick up
another exciting Specialist story
from Debra Webb!
Look for* HER HIDDEN TRUTH
coming from Harlequin Intrigue.

Turn the page for an exciting preview!

MISSION BRIEFING

Thomas Casey reviewed the file in his hand once more before he began the priority one briefing with his deputy, Lucas Camp. This one was going to be a little sticky and a lot dangerous to the specialist assigned to the case.

"That bad, is it?"

Casey glanced up. Lucas read him too easily. He didn't like that. No one else had ever been able to analyze him as well as Lucas could. Though they had worked together only for a short time, since Jack Raine brought down the former director of Special Ops, who sold out his field operatives on a regular basis, Lucas had earned Casey's respect up front.

The man knew his business.

Mission Recovery involved a great deal more than merely the spy business, the unit's sole purpose was to salvage missions gone bad for other agencies. Sometimes simply spying was the goal, other times it was infiltrating the enemy—becoming one of them really—and bringing them down from the inside.

As was the case with the one the CIA had just passed to Mission Recovery and its team of specialists.

"That bad," Casey agreed finally, allowing his deputy the pleasure of knowing he'd read him yet again. "Katrina Moore." Casey opened the file and leaned back in his chair. "CIA Shadow Ops. Twenty-seven years old—"

Lucas swore. "What's a kid like that doing in Shadow Ops? When I ran things over there, only seasoned operatives were allowed in that club."

Casey had wondered the same thing, but that wasn't his problem. "Fluent in several languages," he went on. "Demolitions expert. Her mission was to infiltrate the World Security Agency's newest team of recruits. And she's the first to field-test the CIA's new profile memory implant."

"Don't those lunatics ever give up? We've been on to WSA for years." Lucas lifted a skeptical eyebrow. "Now, the implant business, that's something new. What've they come up with this time?"

Casey laid the file aside and repeated what he'd learned that morning about the CIA's newest gadget. "It's a tiny computer chip surgically implanted in the brain where memory is stored. When an operative is under deep cover and feels that his or her cover is in jeopardy, the implant can be quickly and easily activated. Once activated the operative's own memory is blocked and replaced by the cover profile."

"Thus the operative becomes the person profiled in his or her cover," Lucas guessed.

Casey nodded. "Drugs, not even torture will make

the operative admit anything other than the cover contained in the implant."

"So what's the problem?" Lucas sat up a little straighter, his interest definitely piqued.

"Either Ms. Moore's implant has malfunctioned or her cover is in serious jeopardy. They want us to send someone in to attempt a retrieval."

"What qualifications do we need?" Lucas asked, no doubt already mentally running down the list of specialists not currently on assignment.

"We only have one choice. Ferrelli."

"Ferrelli? Why's that?"

Casey nodded. "He's part of her implant profile."

"These two have a history?"

"Apparently," Casey affirmed.

Lucas said derisively. "I hope the boys in the Company built in a back door for this nifty little gray-matter gadget."

Casey stroked his chin, worry nagging at him. Personal involvement was never a good thing. It could get a man killed. He didn't believe in sending his specialists into a situation he felt less than comfortable with—but he had little choice.

"There's a code phrase," he said in answer to Lucas's question. "All Ferrelli has to do is get in and say the code phrase and she'll recognize him as the former lover she's still hung up on. The implant will automatically imprint his connection to her into memory."

"Assuming the damned thing is functioning properly," Lucas interjected.

"Yes," Casey acknowledged.

Lucas sighed. "Ferrelli's good." He considered the matter a moment then nodded resolutely. "He can handle the situation. Even if it is personal."

"If the implant malfunctions," Casey reminded, though he knew that Lucas was fully aware of what he was about to say, "we'll be sending him into a death trap."

Their gazes locked. Lucas's gray eyes held a lifetime of wisdom, an entire career of confidence and plain old guts—the kind only gained by experience. "That's why they've called on us. We're the best and all other efforts have failed. They know we won't."

"They're right," Casey agreed. "We won't." Katrina Moore was counting on them, he didn't add.

"Let's go into this briefing with Ferrelli without giving away that we know about their history," Casey suggested.

Lucas shrugged. "All right. I see your point. We need to know just how personal this is."

"His initial reaction, yes," Casey said. "I need to be sure the risk isn't too great."

Casey could always count on Lucas. Mission Recovery was extremely lucky to have him. As optimistic as Lucas was about the success of this upcoming mission, something was not quite right. It was apparently personal since Lucas had not chosen to share it with him. That really didn't bother Casey since his and Lucas's personal relationship was only in the beginning stages. What did concern him, however, was the Colby Agency connection. Casey had gleaned from Lucas's frequent trips to Chicago that Victoria Colby was more than a friend. Whatever was troubling Lucas involved this Victoria Colby. Though Lucas hadn't asked for his help, Casey had every intention of looking into the matter.

"Anything else?" Lucas asked, his finely tuned radar picking up Casey's thoughts.

Casey shook his head. "That's all for now."

Lucas stood and reached for his cane. "I'll start pulling together the mission profile." He grinned as if all were well in his world. "We mustn't keep the CIA waiting."

COMING NEXT MONTH

#697 HER HIDDEN TRUTH by Debra Webb
The Specialists
When CIA agent Katrina Moore's memory implant malfunctioned while she was under deep cover, her only hope for rescue lay with Vince Ferrelli. Only, Kat and Vince shared a tumultuous past, which threatened to sabotage their mission. Could Vince save Kat—and restore her memories—before it was too late?

#698 HEIR TO SECRET MEMORIES by Mallory Kane
Top Secret Babies
After he was brutally attacked and left for dead, Jay Wellcome lost all of his memories. His only recollection: the image of a nameless beauty. And though Jay never anticipated they'd come face-to-face, when Paige Reynolds claimed she needed him—honor demanded he offer his protection. Paige's daughter had been kidnapped and nothing would stop him from tracking a killer—especially when he learned her child was also his....

#699 THE ROOKIE by Julie Miller
The Taylor Clan
For the youngest member of the Taylor clan, Josh Taylor, an undercover assignment to smoke out drug dealers on a university campus could promote him to detective. Only, Josh never anticipated his overwhelming feelings for his pregnant professor Rachel Livesay. And when the single mother-to-be's life was threatened by a stalker named "Daddy," Josh's protective instincts took over. But would Rachel accept his protection...and his love?

#700 CONFESSIONS OF THE HEART by Amanda Stevens
Fully recovered from her heart transplant surgery, Anna Sebastian was determined to start a new life. But someone was determined to thwart her plans.... With her life in jeopardy, tough-as-nails cop Ben Porter was the only man she could trust. And now in a race against time, could Ben and Anna uncover the source of the danger before she lost her second chance?

Visit us at www.eHarlequin.com

HARLEQUIN®
INTRIGUE®

brings you the next installment in
Julie Miller's popular series!

KANSAS CITY'S FINEST
BELONGS TO ONE FAMILY—
THE TAYLOR CLAN

It was only supposed to be a routine assignment, but
one that could earn him the badge of detective—infiltrate
a drug ring on a prominent college campus. However,
Josh Taylor never expected to fall for his beautiful, older
and *pregnant* professor, Rachel Livesay. Now Rachel's baby
is threatened by the sperm donor who vows to snatch
the newborn child from Rachel's arms. When Josh's
investigation intersects with Rachel's deadly stalker,
sparks of suspense—and passion—will fly!

THE ROOKIE
February 2003

*Available at your
favorite retail outlet.*

HARLEQUIN®
Makes any time special ®

HARLEQUIN®
INTRIGUE®

Opens the case files on:

Unwrap the mystery!

January 2003
THE SECRET SHE KEEPS
BY CASSIE MILES

February 2003
HEIR TO
SECRET MEMORIES
BY MALLORY KANE

March 2003
CLAIMING HIS FAMILY
BY ANN VOSS PETERSON

Follow the clues to your favorite retail outlet!